My Girlfriend's a GEEK

v2.0

Pentabu

Yen
Press
NEW YORK

My Girlfriend's a Geek
Volume 2

WEL-
COME
TO THE
ROTTEN
WORLD
OF FU-
JOSHI!

Date:

GRA PENTABU V.2
Pentabu.
My girlfriend's a geek.

LOOKING BACK...
PART 2.
2006/12/07 20:20 *01#

MY GIRLFRIEND'S
A GEEK.
PART 2.
2006/12/08 20:00 *08#

BOOKSHELVES.
2006/12/10 14:25 *14#

TSUNDERE (?) TALK.
2006/12/12 16:59 *20#

GENERATION GAP.
2006/12/13 23:29 *26#

SHARING AN
UMBRELLA.
2006/12/15 17:45 *34#

HONEY AND
CLOVER.
2006/12/17 23:34 *38#

DORAEMON.
2006/12/18 20:48 *43#

SUIT.
2006/12/23 23:07 *49#

CHRISTMAS.
2006/12/27 20:40 *55#

SILLY CHAT FROM
A SILLY COUPLE.
2006/12/29 21:10 *65#

TAKING MY
GIRLFRIEND TO
MEET MY PARENTS.
2007/01/02 18:40 *73#

TAKING MY
GIRLFRIEND TO
MEET MY PARENTS.
PART 2.
2007/01/04 20:14 *76#

TAKING MY
GIRLFRIEND TO
MEET MY PARENTS.
PART 3.
2007/01/12 22:55 *84#

TAKING MY
GIRLFRIEND TO
MEET MY PARENTS.
PART 4.
2007/01/21 20:13 *93#

MY GIRLFRIEND'S A GEEK Volume 2

PENTABU

Translation: Stephen Paul

My Girlfriend's a Geek Vol. 2 © 2007 PENTABU. All Rights reserved. First published in Japan in 2007 by ENTERBRAIN, INC., Tokyo. English translation rights arranged with ENTERBRAIN, INC. through Tuttle-Mori Agency, Inc., Tokyo.

English translation © 2011 by Hachette Book Group, Inc.

Yen Press

Hachette Book Group

237 Park Avenue, New York, NY 10017

www.HachetteBookGroup.com

www.YenPress.com

Yen Press is an imprint of Hachette Book Group, Inc. The Yen Press name and logo are trademarks of Hachette Book Group, Inc.

First Yen Press Edition: March 2011

Library of Congress Cataloging-in-Publication Data

Pentabu.
   [Fujoshi kanojo. English]
   My girlfriend's a geek / Pentabu ; [translated by Stephen Paul]. —1st Yen Press ed.
      v. <1> cm.
   Summary: A college student falls in love with a "fangirl"—an obsessive comic and cartoon fan—who introduces him to her cult-like interests, which he reports on his blog.
   ISBN 978-0-7595-3171-0 (v. 1) — ISBN 978-0-7595-3172-7 (v. 2)
   [1. Interpersonal relations—Fiction.   2. Dating (Social customs)—Fiction.   3. Cartoons and comics—Fiction.   4. Blogs—Fiction.   5. Japan—Fiction.]   I. Paul, Stephen.   II. Title.
III. Title: My girlfriend is a geek.
   PZ7.P3895My 2010
   [Fic]—dc22

2010015688

10 9 8 7 6 5 4 3 2 1

RRD-C

Printed in the United States of America

This blog is a record of battle as dictated

by a man with a fujoshi girlfriend.

Okay, that was a lie. I'm not fighting at all.

The war is purely one-sided. Each day I am

dragged farther and farther into

the world of otaku.

I cannot be held responsible for any damages

incurred by reading this blog and falling

into the same predicament.

There is much otaku talk contained within, so

please follow your directions carefully and do not

exceed your recommended dosage.

Looking
Back... Part 2.

Autumn, several years ago.
An acquaintance of mine showed me a place that was hiring
for a part-time job — where I met my girlfriend, Y-ko.

She had shown she was competent enough to take on a lot
of work despite being so young.
Since we were relatively close in age and often spent time
working together, it didn't take much time at all for us to
grow friendly...

Soon we were going out to eat after work and making
shopping trips together on our days off.

It didn't develop into anything more than a friendship
between the boss and the part-timer until one late, moonlit
night, when we were trudging home after working overtime.

Y-KO:	Look at that! What a beautiful moon.
ME:	It sure is...
	Err, Y-ko?
Y-KO:	Hmm? What?
ME:	May I hold your hand?
Y-KO:	Huh? My hand?

She stared at the hand I was offering, frozen.
Well, that makes sense.
We'd been friendly, but certainly not holding-hands friendly.

ME: Yes, your hand. May I?
Y-KO: ...All right.

I grabbed the hand she reluctantly held out, entwining her
fingers one by one.
My palm was damp with nervous sweat.

Y-KO: ...This makes me feel nervous.
ME: Me, too.
Y-KO: Do you like holding hands?
ME: Yes, I do.
Y-KO: I see.
ME: But more than that...

Here, I stopped both my sentence and my gait.
An instant later, she stopped walking as well.
She turned around, looking up at me with her head tilted.

Our eyes met.

Y-KO: ...Yes?
ME: ...I like you.
Y-KO: ...Huh?
ME: May I kiss you?

My empty left hand traced her cheek.

She closed her eyes.

Several moments later, after our lips broke contact, we looked into each other's eyes again.

Y-KO: ...I just want to tell you one thing first.
ME: ......What is it?
Y-KO: **I'm an otaku. Is that okay with you?**
ME: ...Huh?
Y-KO: ...Actually, in my case,
               I'm what's known as a **fujoshi**...so...are you weirded out?
ME: Uh, no. I'm just surprised. I would never have thought you were...
Y-KO: Well, I keep it a secret from other people...
ME: ...So, what about it?
Y-KO: Huh?
ME: What's the connection between me liking you, and the fact that you're an otaku or a fujoshi or whatever?
Y-KO: Um...
ME: **I like you a lot, and it has nothing to do with what you call yourself.**

And it was true.
It didn't matter to me whether she was an otaku or not.

Y-KO: ...Um, thanks.
ME: Would you be my girlfriend?
Y-KO: ....Sure. I'd love to.

And as she said this, she smiled shyly.

But at the time, I had no idea what she meant by the word *fujoshi*.

And that's where we left off in the previous volume. But there is more to this tale...

ME: By the way, Y-ko...
Y-KO: What is it, boyfriend?

You don't have to refer to me as "boyfriend."
It's a bit embarrassing...but that's not my point.

ME: You mentioned the word, uh, **fujoshi** earlier.
                What is that?
Y-KO: ......Pardon?
ME: I mean, I don't really understand what **fujoshi**
                means...
Y-KO: ......**Pardon?**

She froze.

Y-KO: ......What? Hang on a moment.
                You mean **you said it was okay with-
                out knowing what fujoshi meant?**
ME: Well, er, yes...
Y-KO: You idiot!
                How many times have I told you at work to
                ask right on the spot if there's anything you

don't understand?! Why would you approve
something like that without understanding
what it means?!

ME: ...?! I...I'm sorry.

Y-KO: Well, you can't turn back now and say, "Sorry,
             it doesn't count now." Got that?!

I don't know what's going on, but I do know that she is mad!

But if I was the one who asked her out, why is the issue here about my approval?

Plus.

ME: ...Look, it's not like I care so little about you
             that this **fujoshi** whatever is going to change
             my mind.

Y-KO: Well...thank you.

ME: No problem. Now, since I don't know, I will ask.
             What is a **fujoshi**?

Y-KO: ...Err, well...

She fudged her speech and clearly averted her eyes from
mine.
...Well, this is obviously not going to make the issue any
easier!

ME: Is this **fujoshi** thing really that big of a deal?

Y-KO: ...Don't freak out when you hear it, okay?

ME: I won't freak out, and of course, I won't hate
             you for it. I promise.

Y-KO: ......

ME: ......

Y-KO: ...Well, a **fujoshi** is —

...a **fujoshi** is?

Y-KO: **— a girl who enjoys romance between a boy and another boy.**

......

A girl who enjoys romance between a boy and another boy.

.........Come again?

ME: ......A boy and another boy?

Y-KO: ...You're looking like you don't get it.

ME: Huh? Oh, sorry.

Y-KO: Okay, it basically means I like **BL — boy's love**.

ME: ...So you're saying you like gay guys?

Y-KO: Oh, go ahead, be blunt about it! It's not really exactly the same thing...
But I guess that would be the simple way of describing it.

ME: ....So, er, you're saying it's not that you like gay characters?

Y-KO: That's not exactly it. Here's an example: Kira and Athrun.
Traditionally, Kira is paired with Lacus and Athrun with Cagalli, but in my case, Kira and Athrun are a couple.

That would be labeled **Kira x Ath.**
. . . You see? I like this sort of BL manga and whatnot.

* Kira Yamato (♂ Earth Alliance) x Lacus Clyne (♀ ZAFT),
Athrun Zala (♂ ZAFT) x Cagalli Yula Athha (♀ Orb Union) are
the primary pairings.
In Y-ko's case, it is Kira (♂) x Athrun (♂).
From *Mobile Suit Gundam SEED*.

. . . . . . Sigh.
I think I understand, but I also think I don't.

ME:	. . . Uh, hang on . . . **Kira x Ath?**
	Those two get paired together . . . ?
Y-KO:	. . . Look, don't think too hard about it, okay?
	It's not really all that serious of a topic . . .
	As long as you understand that I like that sort of stuff, that's all you need to know.
ME:	Oh . . . I see . . . Okay, got it.
Y-KO:	So . . . are you weirded out? Are you okay?
ME:	. . . Huh? Yeah, I think I'm fine.
	So, you're saying that it's not like you prefer someone whose profile I don't match?
Y-KO:	Huh? Well, yeah.
ME:	Well, then there's no problem.

Whew! That's great.
I don't know what I'd do if she suddenly told me I wasn't right for her.

Y-KO:	......Are you sure you want me?
ME:	Of course. What did I just say? **I love you, and it has nothing to do with being an otaku or fujoshi.**
Y-KO:	...Okay. Thanks. I...I love you, too.

And so,
on an autumn night, beneath a beautiful moon...
our relationship became that of boyfriend and girlfriend, and
she became...

my **geeky girlfriend.**

My Girlfriend's a Geek, Part 2.

`2006/12/08 20:00`

My girlfriend is a fujoshi.
I'm sure that many of you have never heard this word before
and don't know what it means.
It's difficult to convey just what a fujoshi is with a simple

explanation, so I'm going to avoid laying out a thorough and precise definition...

In my girlfriend's case, she loves anime and manga and knows a lot about them.
In that way, I guess you could say she's an otaku.
Plus.

This is a big part of what makes a fujoshi...

* Roy x Ed: A pairing involving two characters from *Hagaren,* or *Fullmetal Alchemist* — the protagonist, Edward Elric (♂), and the Flame Alchemist, Roy Mustang (♂).

...Just like this.

A fujoshi obsesses over romance between a male character and another male character.

This blog, "My Girlfriend's a Geek Part 2,"
follows my everyday life with just such a girlfriend.

Now, then.

It's been a little over two years since I began my relationship with this fujoshi.

When we first started going out, it was like this.

Y-KO:	Hey, read this!
ME:	…? What is it?
Y-KO:	I recommend this manga. It's great.
ME:	Okay. Let's see… **Wha —?!**
	Is it just me, or does this seem a bit sexual?
Y-KO:	By the way —
ME:	…Huh?
Y-KO:	**In the later parts, it's completely sexual.**
ME:	…What?!
Y-KO:	Aha-ha-ha! Your face is all red.
ME:	Wha —! N-no, it's not!
Y-KO:	So, spill the beans. What were you just imagining?
ME:	Oh, shut up!!

......
As you can see, I was constantly on the losing side.
But these days, now that we've been together for two years…

Y-KO:	Hey, the new volume of *Nana* is out.
ME:	Oh, cool.
Y-KO:	This one will fulfill all your expectations for sexiness.

ME: That's not really what I expect out of it, but
     whatever...
     Funny how shōjo manga seems to have more
     sex than shōnen manga...

Y-KO: I think you're right.

ME: Well, I am interested in seeing what happens
     next, and I'm old enough not to make a big
     deal out of a little eroticism.

Y-KO: Oh yeah? But **BL is a lot sexier.**

— BL (Boy's Love) books.
Where male characters fall in love with each other.

By the way, many of the publications Y-ko owns are not for
minors.

ME: ...Yes, I suppose so.

They probably earn that eighteen-and-up rating.
...But so what if your BL stuff is sexy? What's your point,
Y-ko?

Y-KO: Wanna see? You're a guy, and guys like sex,
     right?
     Here, I recommend this one! Go on, take a
     look!

I looked at the BL book thrust into my face.
On the cover, I already saw two men clinging to each other
and looking at me.

Dammit, don't look at me like that.

ME:	Y-ko...
Y-KO:	Hmm? What is it, Sebas?
ME:	...If I start reading that book now, **I won't be able to prepare dinner.** **Oh, unless you wanted instant noodles tonight?**
Y-KO:	.........!!

Yes.
For the most part, breakfast and dinner are my responsibility.
This isn't necessarily because I'm a good cook.
It's because she's a working woman and I'm still a student,
and over time this simply became our common practice.

ME:	......
Y-KO:	......In-**instant noodles**...
ME:	Oh, and we don't have any at home, so you'll have to go out and buy some.
Y-KO:	Ugh.........!!
ME:	......
Y-KO:	......**Please prepare our supper.**
ME:	Understood, madam.

A nice, clean escape.
...In a case like this, if I answer truthfully with

"I'm only interested in *girls* doing sexy things!
I don't care about *guys* doing them!"

Y-ko responds with

"Oh well, if they **turn into women,** you're okay with it?!
In fact, I'm guessing you'd be okay as long as they look like women, right?!
I've got some of those! Here, look at this!!
From a distance, this person looks just like a girl (only with the usual package attached)**!!**
Go on, read it!!"

...And then the argument is all but lost (speaking from experience).

* Turn into women: A fictional situation in which a man's body suddenly turns female. How strange!
Through this event, where one member becomes a woman, the usual gay "uke x seme" dynamic turns into a traditional heterosexual relationship.

As you might guess,
I've learned to shoot for an easy escape most of the time.
...There's no way to win when you face Y-ko head-on.

Of course, after two years of undergoing this hazing,
a guy manages to pick up a trick or two to combat it.

Y-KO: Damn!
               Give me back the younger,
               sweeter you!!

ME: Sorry, Y-ko...

But you are totally stealing my line.

You're the one who made me that way.
...Not that I particularly regret it.

Book-shelves.

2006/12/10 14:25

It was two years ago that I met Y-ko.
She was my boss at the job I was working at the time.

I was a student, and I had no idea what I was doing.
In order to learn how to do my job properly,
I had no choice but to speak with her regularly in the
workplace.

After a time, we ended up becoming boyfriend and
girlfriend.

It turned out she was a fujoshi.
Not only that, but a **hidden fujoshi**,
one who didn't show any inkling of her nature around other people...
But as a general rule, she never hides this around me.

In fact...
It seems more like she's intent on dragging me down that path with her.

...And I'll be honest.
It's slowly but surely seeping into me.

This story is from a day when she came to visit me at my house.
At my house.

Y-ko stares intently at my bookshelf.

ME:	...What are you looking at?
Y-KO:	Hmm? Oh, I was just checking to see if *My Girlfriend's a Geek* is really in here.
ME:	...Didn't I tell you I would put it on my shelf?
Y-KO:	Yeah. Well, at least you're a bit more otaku-ish now.
	Of course, you've got a long way to go.
ME:	...Long way to go?
Y-KO:	I mean, come on.
	Shouldn't a normal college student's bookshelf have way more manga on it?

ME: That's quite a weird stereotype to hold...

Y-KO: Where's the *Strawberry 100%* and the *Love Hina* and the *Negima*?

ME: That's ridiculous! Where do you get these ideas?

Those are all manga that have a ton of girls in them!

If you were going to imagine a college student's bookshelf packed full of manga, at least throw out some titles like *Dragon Ball* or *Slam Dunk*!

Y-KO: And all these novels...Haruki Murakami and Takayoshi Honda.
I know they're good and all...but don't you have anything a bit studentlike?

ME: Well, I do have *Twelve Kingdoms*...
and *Angel's Egg*. They made a movie out of that.

Y-KO: That's not what I mean! I'm saying, throw some light novels in there!
The kind of stuff I can read when you're too busy cooking to pay attention to me!

Light novels...? Oh, those young adult novels.
True, Y-ko strikes me as more of a NisiOisin person than Yuka Murayama.

And come on, Y-ko.

ME: ...And there's no option for helping me cook...?

Y-KO: How can I? Your kitchen's too small.

ME: Okay, good point...

So, you would help if it was bigger?
Then why am I always the only one cooking at your place, too?!

...Of course, being a student, I've got a lot more free time to spend cooking than Y-ko.

Y-KO: I mean, like the *Haruhi Suzumiya* series.
                I want you to get light novels that I would like.

ME: Oh, I was thinking of buying that. It sounds like it's a huge hit.

Y-KO: Really?!

ME: Yes, I actually went to the bookstore to buy it.

Y-KO: So did you buy it!? I...I don't see it on your shelf.

ME: The first volume was sold out, so I couldn't. So I bought a different book instead.

Haruhi sure is popular.
It makes me jealous.

Y-KO: Hmm...So what did you buy instead of *Haruhi?* The *Zaregoto* series?
                Or maybe a BL novel? Heh-heh, then I'd forgive you.

ME: Let's see...It was...aha. Here it is.

* *Zaregoto* series: NisiOisin's debut work, starting with the
Kubikiri Cycle (winner of Kodansha's Mephisto Award).
Spans nine works collected into six titles.

I pulled out the book I bought on that trip and handed it to
Y-ko.

Y-KO:	Hmm, let's see...
ME:	It's pretty good. Want to borrow it?
Y-KO:	... **The Definitive How to Truly Understand Economic Analysis**...?
ME:	Yep. I found the concept of net-operating profit to be really interesting.
Y-KO:	Okay... **but what happened to the light novels?!** This is a textbook!! How can you possibly consider *this* to be a replacement for *Haruhi*?!
ME:	Well, that kind of depends on how you see it. Think of it as a light novel. You'll burn through it in no time.
Y-KO:	No I won't! And how can you put light novels and textbooks on the same level?!
ME:	That's a strange question... Anyways, this is all thanks to you. If I hadn't met you, I wouldn't have discovered the option of buying light novels.

That and this isn't a textbook.
If anything, it's a how-to book.

Y-KO: ...Are you saying that if you weren't going out with me, you wouldn't even have considered the choice of light novels?!

It's not the "reading" part as much as the "buying" part...
...Yeah, I'm guessing I wouldn't.
So it does all come down to her influence.

ME: Yeah, I guess that's right...
Y-KO: And when you buy books, you would have always bought books like this?!
         Y-you've gotta be joking!!

Y-KO: And of all things, net-operating profit?!
         — I've got it!

You're into that **net-operating profit moe,** aren't you?!
If you're getting turned on by abstract concepts, then there's nothing left for me to teach!

ME: Don't talk about that like it's some natural conclusion!!
It's not like I have some kind of extraordinary sexual taste!!

Y-KO: Oh, really? Too bad...

I guess we'll just have to work on developing that together!!

ME: Uh, would you stop trying to run in the wrong direction?!

...Answer me.

— To exactly *what* kind of world are you trying to take me?!

Tsundere (?) Talk.

2006/12/12 16:59

A whim often refers to something that pops up completely out of the blue, but Y-ko has an uncanny ability to imagine things out of thin air that far exceeds the trappings of this concept.

She takes that idea and carefully — no, carelessly — considers it in her head, and if the meeting of the mind confirms that it will be in any way "entertaining"...

...she gets me involved without hesitation.

So, here we go.
Another idiotic conversation between me and Y-ko.

Y-KO:	**From now on, I think I'll try to be a tsundere. For your sake.**
ME:	...I see. For my sake?
Y-KO:	To start off: Hurry up and make dinner, Sebas!
ME:	How is that any different from normal? Plus, if we're alone together, shouldn't you be hanging all over me rather than yelling?
Y-KO:	Hmph...W-well, it's not like I'm doing it for your sake!
ME:	Doing what?!
Y-KO:	Trying to be a tsundere.
ME:	**You're spectacularly contradicting yourself!!**

Plus, that's the kind of thing you say to hide your embarrassment after someone calls you out!
You don't just say "I'm not doing it for your sake" out of the blue...**I think!** (worried)

Y-KO:	Spectacular...? D-don't expect me to say **thanks for that compliment!**
ME:	Spectacularly is an adverb, and I wasn't complimenting you.

Y-KO:	Why not? You should!
ME:	For what?!

Tsundere sure are annoying!
No, wait — it's just Y-ko.
…Hmm?
Hang on, me. Settle down. Besides —

ME:	Besides, Y-ko…You know that tsundere don't turn me on to begin with, right?
Y-KO:	…Huh? They don't…?
ME:	Yes. So saying that you want to be a tsundere "for my sake" doesn't make any sense…
Y-KO:	Hmm…Whatever, then.
ME:	You're going to keep doing it?! I think you're really missing the point!
Y-KO:	Well, as long as me being a tsundere turns me on, I don't care.
ME:	So, it's some kind of self-stimulation? Or should I say, **self-stimoetion**?
Y-KO:	You might call it **self-moefficiency**.
ME:	Okay, so assuming you're all set with that… What's my role in all of this?
Y-KO:	Your role is Villager A.
ME:	That sounds like a really minor role!
Y-KO:	Not happy? Fine, I'll be generous…You can also have Villager B.
ME:	How is that generous in any way?
Y-KO:	Oh, and you don't have any dialogue.
ME:	Then what's the point of me appearing at all?

Y-KO:	Oh, there's a meaning. That's right...The two villagers are old friends. Friendship between the two men blossoms into love, and that means a love scene. That's when the drama really begins to thicken.
ME:	All this without any dialogue...? **And why does it have to be two men?**
Y-KO:	Don't worry about the dialogue. All you need to do is *receive.* Got a problem?
ME:	What I have can't be expressed with the word *problem*!!
Y-KO:	Oh, stop shouting. You'll bother the neighbors, Sebas.
ME:	If you're going to be a tsundere, at least try to show a bit of the -*dere!*

Too much tsun.
How is anyone supposed to find this a turn-on?
I should sue you for misleading advertising.

Y-KO:	Who cares? Even Fanta Grape doesn't have any fruit juice.
ME:	...Pardon?
Y-KO:	I can be a tsundere with zero percent dere.
ME:	But Fanta still tastes like grape...

Even if it's just chemicals and artificial coloring.
And what do you mean, **zero percent dere**?
It's just tsun!

Is a mere tsun all you are!?

Y-KO:	**Dere content is simulated. Actual me will vary.**
ME:	I wish you wouldn't lie about the most important part of the equation! **And I thought the dere was supposed to be the best part of tsundere!**
Y-KO:	The crafty hawk hides its talons.
ME:	...Okay.
Y-KO:	**The tsundere Y-ko abandons her dere.**
ME:	If you have to throw out a part, get rid of the tsun! And if you can't do that, at least hide the dere rather than abandoning it!
Y-KO:	**You sound so desperate about this, Sebas... Gasp! Unless —!** You're actually a fan of tsundere? A ***tsundeler***?!
ME:	I've never even heard of that word before!!
Y-KO:	It's the latest craze in linguistic innovation!
ME:	No, it's not!
Y-KO:	You make a pretty cool tsundra!!
ME:	Tundra? Am I supposed to be a fan of arctic wasteland!?

Tundra moe?
How the hell does anyone get turned on by that?
Latest craze of linguistic desecration is more like it.

Y-KO:	...So you really want me to be that lovey-dovey?
ME:	No, it's just...Oh, hell. Fine, let's just say I do.
Y-KO:	All right, then. Are you familiar with the term **equal exchange**, Sebas?
ME:	...And what must I do to earn an equal measure of dere?
Y-KO:	Ten shoulder massages.
ME:	That's cheap! Wow, your dere is easy to buy!! If it was that easy, you should just do that to start with...
Y-KO:	Hey, don't be rude! You have no idea how valuable your massages are to me. You don't know what a pleasure they are, so don't tell me they're cheap. **Your shoulder massages are the most relaxing thing in the world...**
ME:	......
Y-KO:	......
ME:	....
Y-KO:	.........I...
ME:	...........I?

Uhhh.

...Right.

— This isn't half bad.

ME:	Y-ko...
Y-KO:	What?!
ME:	Shall I massage your shoulders?

Y-KO: Why are you smirking at me like that? I'm not that — **Oh!!**

Not bad.
Not bad at all.

Generation Gap.

2006/12/13 23:29

So, here we go.
At Y-ko's place.
A conversation held while we were pulling an all-nighter, doing work.

Y-KO: ... How do you read this, Sebas?

She pointed out a particular kanji to me.

ME: Y-ko, I think you ought to be able to read this one...
Y-KO: Shut up, relaxed generation!
ME: Actually, I think I was just a few years before the relaxed generation...

Plus, even if I was a member of that generation,
wouldn't that mean your own vocabulary is even smaller?
Or wait, this isn't even about vocabulary, is it? It's more
like...literacy?
...Maybe my own vocabulary is in trouble.

Y-KO: If you didn't have to go to school on
Saturdays, you're in the relaxed generation!
ME: ...Wouldn't that mean you're in that
generation, too...?
Y-KO: ......
ME: ......
Y-KO: ...Well, being in the relaxed generation is
kind of stylish, wouldn't you say?
ME: That was a startling about-face.

See how fast she turns around?
You're like the tsundere heroine of NisiOisin's
Bakemonogatari.
The one who makes fun of the protagonist's mountain bike.

Y-KO: So stylish, it's almost like...relaxed-ish.
ME: Relaxed-ish!?
That was not clever enough to warrant the
smug look on your face right now!
Y-KO: **Silence, Sebas-ish.**
ME: Stop combining them!

Not only did that sound terrible, but it sounds hard to
pronounce!

Y-KO:	...So anyways, Sebash-ish —
ME:	That didn't take long to screw up!
Y-KO:	...So anyways, Sebash —
ME:	You tried again, but you still can't say it right.
Y-KO:	Look there, Sebash...I can see van Gogh's painting above you.
ME:	Are you saying I'm about to die!?

Is she angry at me?!
Plus, wouldn't that mean her *own* death is imminent?!
And wasn't it a Rubens painting, not van Gogh?!

...Hang on, this joke's probably a bit too old for you folks, isn't it?

* Rubens painting: In the last episode of *A Dog of Flanders,* Nero and his dog Patrasche froze to death underneath a painting by Flemish painter Peter Paul Rubens.

Y-KO:	Anyways, Sebsh.
ME:	...You're completely tongue-tied by now.
Y-KO:	Well, it's quite a tongue twister.
ME:	Not particularly...but you're certainly making it into one.
Y-KO:	No, it really is a tongue tistwer —
ME:	You just did it again!

There's that *Bakemonogatari* again! This time you're like the little kid ghost who can't pronounce anything right! And sadly, you're more than twice her age!

Y-KO:	Hmm…It's not working.
	How can we pull off really fun conversations like in *Bakemonogatari*?
ME:	I dunno. I think we're doing a pretty good job already…
Y-KO:	Really? Then can I cuss you out like the heroine, Senjōgahara?
ME:	Please don't…I don't think my ego could handle it…

I'm not as tough as the protagonist in that book.
I just can't survive that withering storm of brutal insults.

Y-KO:	Oh, fine. **Should we just go with the usual BL talk?**
ME:	What do you mean, the usual?!
	That makes it sound like I willingly discuss BL with you all the time!
Y-KO:	Oh, don't worry. The night is long!
ME:	Sorry, it's nearly sunrise!
	And I haven't gotten anywhere with this!
Y-KO:	Sunrise…Speaking of that, how about *Azure Before the Sunrise*?
	We can talk about that!
ME:	*Azure Before the*…? Wh-what is that?
Y-KO:	You don't know about *Azure Before the Sunrise*? Well, it's…
ME:	…It's?
Y-KO:	**An adult computer game.**
ME:	What exactly do you expect from me?!

On what basis does she assume that I would know about that?
And assuming I was familiar with it,
why would you want me to have played it before, Y-ko?!

Y-KO:	You haven't heard of it? But it's common knowledge!
ME:	Says who?! Your standards of "common knowledge" are way out of whack!
Y-KO:	You should know everything that's been turned into an anime!
ME:	That's crazy! You have some really unreasonable expectations of me!

And this thing was animated?
There sure are a lot of anime based on eroge...
Even Y-ko's favorite, *Fate/stay night*, was animated.

Y-KO:	Of course, it'd be years before a total novice like you could hold a decent conversation about this way of life with a master like myself.
ME:	Are you proud of that fact?

And to what "way of life" are you referring? Erotic computer games?
...And you're a master at them?
I learn something new every day...

Y-KO:	And now you must master your own way of life.

ME:	What's that?
Y-KO:	The ways of carnality.
ME:	Pardon?
Y-KO:	**I'm talking about sodomy.**

Sodomy...
The real-life version of BL!!

ME:	I have absolutely zero intention of setting foot on that path, much less mastering it!
Y-KO:	**Blaze down the path, Sebas!**
ME:	Are you speeding this up?
Y-KO:	Yes, acceleration... There's an acceleration device on the inside of your wisdom tooth.
ME:	...Acceleration device?

What is she talking about?
Damn, I don't recognize whatever it is she's referencing...
Hmmm... What story is likely to have an acceleration device
in it...?

ME:	What am I supposed to be... Hyuuma... Hoshi?

...It was a weak, doubtful comeback.

Y-KO:	Why would there be an acceleration device in *Star of the Giants*?!

She came back on my comeback!

I should have known I would fail that one!

ME: Doesn't he, like...try to steal a ton of
            bases...?
Y-KO: **Star of the Giants is about how Hyuuma
            Hoshi's father tries to turn him into a
            perfect baseball player, not a perfect
            baseball cyborg!!
            The wisdom tooth acceleration device is
            from *Cyborg 009*!
            Get it together!!**

But I don't know anything about *Cyborg* 009...
Damn! My lack of knowledge was pitifully exposed on that
one...
Maybe she was right about me being a total novice!

Y-KO: Heh...If you have to curse anything, curse
            your own ignorance.
            I think you should start with the basics. *Astro
            Boy* should be a good launching pad.
            Oh, and bonus points if you memorize the
            years involved.
ME: ...The years...?

This conversation has turned into a history lesson...
...And give me a break.

Cyborg 009.
Manga serialized in 1964.

Star of the Giants.
Manga serialized in 1966.

...Is there any wonder someone my age wouldn't know about these things?
— So how are you so familiar with them, Y-ko...?

What I'm feeling now isn't my lack of knowledge, but the generation gap between us.

...But I still know all about *A Dog of Flanders* (aired in 1975)...
I guess it's just something that varies from person to person.

Sharing an Umbrella.

`2006/12/15 17:45`

In the rain.

Two of us under one umbrella.
Just another shared umbrella conversation.

Y-KO: Oh boy, it's really coming down now.
ME: It sure is...You want to find someplace we
            can duck inside?
Y-KO: Mm, nah, let's just go home...I
            kind of like sharing the umbrella
            like this.
ME: You do?
Y-KO: Yeah. It feels good having our shoulders
            touch like this.
            ...It's a tight squeeze, but you still make sure
            I don't get rained on.
ME: Oh, it's not that big of a deal, really...
Y-KO: Thanks. I love the little things you do
            for me.

...Wh-what's going on?

There's a strong feeling in the air...

Is this the moment where I should whisper my own words of love back to her?

ME:	Y-ko —
Y-KO:	So as thanks, how about I let you **read all of my BL material you want?**
ME:	**— I will firmly, vehemently decline, thanks.**

Give me back that nice mood of fifteen seconds ago.
Give me back the opportunity to use the words I was considering so very carefully.

Y-KO:	How come? I was sentencing you to all-you-can-read BL! When I show you my appreciation, you ought to accept it gratefully!
ME:	Why do you have to **"sentence"** me to your appreciation?!
Y-KO:	. . . Tch! You're just as picky as you look, Sebas!
ME:	As I look?! You can judge that based on looks?!
Y-KO:	With my mind's eye.
ME:	I thought the mind's eye was supposed to see everything but looks!!

Mind's eye.
It's supposed to look past the exterior to the true nature of things, or so I thought.
Not something that judges outward appearances.

...And what do you mean, I look picky?

Y-KO:	Okay, enough of the jokes... I'm satisfied with life. At night, as well as the morning and afternoon.
ME:	...Sounds like you're satisfied all day long.
Y-KO:	**It's a 24-7, year-round, no holidays kind of love.**
ME:	You make it sound like a convenience store...

That's kind of a mild description
for such a touching sentiment.

Y-KO:	So what about you?
ME:	...Pardon?
Y-KO:	Are you in love with me 24-7, year-round, no holidays?
ME:	.......Uhh, well —
Y-KO:	...You're not.
ME:	...No, that's not true. I'm in love with you 24-7, year-round, no holidays.
Y-KO:	So you're basically in heat.
ME:	That's incorrect!
Y-KO:	So you're practically in heat?
ME:	It's the "in heat" part I am protesting!
Y-KO:	Pssh...Shut your mouth, puberty boy. I can tell these things.
ME:	Wow. Why are you pulling out the older lady card now?

Y-KO:	Why? To hide the fact that I'm in heat!
ME:	Okay, point made. Keep using that older lady card, please...

So, she thinks she's in heat, huh...?

Y-KO:	Oh, come on, I'm only kidding. Don't take it so seriously.
ME:	...Please don't joke like that in broad daylight.
Y-KO:	**What about at night?**
ME:	Is it that important to you?!

...Sigh.

What can I say?

— I thought two lovers sharing an umbrella would have...
...a more romantic mood working, y'know...?

. . . . . .

Honey and Clover.

2006/12/17 23:34

One of my girlfriend's favorite manga is *Honey and Clover*. There's a very distinctive part of the story where one of the characters, Takemoto, takes off on a bicycle and goes around the country on a soul-seeking journey.

On that journey, he meets many different people and grows in a number of ways.
That part of the story apparently really hit Y-ko's sweet spot.

Y-KO: Ahh, I wish I could go on a soul-seeking journey like Takemoto!
ME: Uhh...you do?
Y-KO: Huh? Why do you sound so exasperated?
ME: Well...You don't really strike me as being the Takemoto type.
          If anything, you're closer to Morita...
Y-KO: Morita? Why?
ME: Because he doesn't need to travel to "find himself." He's already got a strong identity. He lives completely by his own whims and fancies without a care in the world...
          I know that's a poor description, but you strike me as the Morita type.

Y-KO:	Really. You think I'm that willful?
ME:	You mean you weren't aware of that...?
Y-KO:	Yeah. I mean, look at how much I want to go on a soul-searching journey! C'mon, Sebas! Let's take a bike ride to Hokkaido!
ME:	Together?! That's not a soul-searching journey, that's a vacation!
Y-KO:	Aww! But I'll get tired of riding my bike. You can pedal, and I'll ride on the back.
ME:	On the back?! What happened to the soul-searching part?! This is turning into a vacation where I do all the work and get tired!!
Y-KO:	Well, don't you like that Ghibli movie, *Whisper of the Heart*? Remember that scene where the boy and girl ride a bike together? Wouldn't you like that? I'll even sing "Take Me Home, Country Roads" rather than "Gandhara." Deal?
ME:	What makes you think I would possibly consider that a **"deal"**...?

I mean, true, I do enjoy "Take Me Home, Country Roads" better than "Gandhara," but still...

Y-KO:	Come on. You're getting twice the bang for your buck. The best parts of both *Honey and Clover* and *Whisper of the Heart*. **Score!**

ME: They're only the best parts for you, and there's zero benefit for *me*!

Y-KO: Oh, fine. Then I'll let you handle the part about writing a BL novel.
Happy now? That's a major episode of the story.

ME: There's nothing even resembling that in either of those stories!
I do remember a part where someone had wild flights of fancy, though!

Y-KO: No way! Doesn't the middle school girl write a novel? I'm pretty sure it'd be a BL —

ME: No, it wouldn't! Stop using yourself as the basis for everything!!

Y-KO: That's kind of rude to say. I made my BL debut in elementary school, you know.

ME: Look...That's not the...

In elementary school? Really?
A bit early to be starting down that path!

Y-KO: ...Oh, fine.
Let's make a huge concession and say that I might be more of the Morita type.

ME: Right.

Y-KO: If I'm supposed to be the Morita type, then what character from *Honey and Clover* do you resemble?

ME: Uhh...I don't really know how to respond to that...

Y-KO: Mario? Luigi maybe?

ME: Why do you pick the weirdest side characters...?

Totally obscure one-off ones, too...
I see...So I'm not cut out to be a protagonist, huh...?

Y-KO: Hmm. Oh I guess you could be Leader, though.

ME: Leader? I don't remember a Leader character.

Y-KO: Sure there was! Remember? **The dog at Fujiwara Design.**

ME: So I'm not even a human being anymore?!

Y-KO: Got a problem with that? At least you're not the **sand from the dunes of Tottori**!

ME: Really?! We're finally sinking to **inanimate objects**?!

Y-KO: Hey, you'd get stepped on by Yamada's beautiful legs!
That's about the most blissful fate you could possibly hope for.

ME: ....

What is this saying about her perspective on my life...?
Being stepped on is the best I can hope for?

Y-KO: Well, jokes aside, you're probably more like Mayama than anyone else.

ME: Aha.

Yes, yes, yes! Mayama, the handsome, stylish, and bespectacled one!
Congratulations, me! I knew I had it in me!

ME:	Mayama, huh? Why's that?
Y-KO:	Well, it's kind of hard to explain, but… How about the fact that he falls in love with a beautiful older woman? Dead giveaway, right?
ME:	……**That's it?**
Y-KO:	Yes. **That's it.**
ME:	………
Y-KO:	Right?
ME:	………

The only similarity is that he fell in love with a beautiful older woman —

…Meaning that…

…the only thing you're really trying to emphasize is that you're a beautiful older woman?!

* "Gandhara" rather than "Take Me Home, Country Roads": While Takemoto was on his journey, he often sang the hit song "Gandhara" by the long-running Japanese band Godiego. In Studio Ghibli's *Whisper of the Heart*, the opening credits were accompanied by Olivia Newton-John's cover of John Denver's "Take Me Home, Country Roads."
* The dunes of Tottori: The place where Ayumi Yamada and Nomiya went on a date in *Honey and Clover*. When Yamada announced she was going back to Tokyo, Nomiya could no longer keep himself from admitting his feelings for her, and they spent a day together. Later, when she finds sand from the dunes spilling out of her shoe, she is reminded of the time she spent with him and feels a sudden twinge of affection. This scene is very famous among *H&C* fans.

Doraemon.

2006/12/18 20:48

Okay.
Everyone's familiar with this iconic show.
Here's a conversation that occured as we watched *Doraemon*.

ME:	Hey, it's *Doraemon*.
Y-KO:	This is one of those shows that is

	surprisingly good when you catch it once in a while.
ME:	Yeah, I guess so...
Y-KO:	...Hey Sebas, what would you think if you were in Doraemon's world?
ME:	What would I think? Probably that it was fun.
Y-KO:	I know, right? **Nobita x Sebas** would probably be great.
ME:	No, it wouldn't! Why can't you think about *fun* things like the Anywhere Door or the bamboo copter?
Y-KO:	Sounds tricky...Would the copter be **seme**?
ME:	Umm...Try to get away from the whole BL thing...

Are there no depths to which you will not sink?
Even mere inanimate *tools* are subject to your fantasies?

Y-KO:	Oh, but imagining you and Nobita involved together is such a turn-on...
ME:	What is your problem?! What's happening to me?!
Y-KO:	And so your innocence wilted as does the flower.
ME:	Excuse me?!
Y-KO:	I tried to make it sound poetic.
ME:	Well, don't! It wasn't that poetic, anyway!

...Not that I really consider myself an expert on poetry.
Anyway...

ME:	...I get the feeling that one person can't possibly have enough comebacks to handle you...

Y-KO:

That means threesome.

ME:	Why?!
Y-KO:	Nobita's gonna have a babe on either side.
ME:	Are you still hung up on that topic?
Y-KO:	Oh, don't worry. We've got a special clause: It doesn't count as cheating if you do it with another man.
ME:	Trust me, if that ever happens, you can count it...

I don't need that idiotic "special" clause.
It's not like I'd ever use it!

Y-KO:	Oh, I can? Then I have you at two, currently.
ME:	Two?!
Y-KO:	...Why? Should it be three?
ME:	It's zero! The number of times I've cheated on you is zero!
Y-KO:	Ha-ha-ha, don't be so silly...
ME:	Why don't you believe me?

Y-KO:	Because I love you!
ME:	Then maybe you should trust me...
Y-KO:	Yes, I'm trusting that you've still only done it twice!
ME:	That's the wrong part to trust in!
Y-KO:	Trust me, don't trust me...What am I to think? **You cat ears–loving bastard!**
ME:	Cat ears?!
Y-KO:	What? Don't you find them to be moe?
ME:	Well, to be perfectly honest, yes... ...but when you scream it at me like an insult, my instinct is to deny it.
Y-KO:	Okay...**you cat-shaped, robot-loving bastard!**
ME:	Nope! That does not get me off!
Y-KO:	Oh, right. I forgot, Doraemon doesn't have any ears.
ME:	Is that what you assumed was my basis for getting turned on?

Even if Doraemon did have cat ears on his head, I wouldn't be getting all hot and bothered!

Y-KO:	You are so picky, Nobita...
ME:	Was that supposed to be an **impression**?! You didn't sound like Doraemon at all!
Y-KO:	W-well, it's only for this one time! You can't always rely on tools to get everything done for you!!

ME: Okay, you can stop trying to make Doraemon
       a moe character now...
Y-KO: Ta-da! **Fluffy handcuffs***.
ME: Why would he have a tool like that?
       What's supposed to be happening to poor
       Nobita?!

What use could you possibly have for handcuffs...?
Sounds like Nobita's in big trouble!

Y-KO: # Use these to torment Sebas to the limit of your desires, Nobita.

ME: **They're for me?!** I'm the one in trouble?!
Y-KO: His skill as a sniper is world-class.
ME: Quite a menacing threat...I'm done for! Help
       me, Doraemon!!
Y-KO: There's no escaping from reality, Sebas! Don't
       avert your eyes from the truth!
ME: It's not reality I want to escape from, it's your
       wicked imagination!
Y-KO: Oh, there's no escape from that. Once you're
       caught, you can never get away.
ME: Sounds terrifying...
Y-KO: **Heh...**

ME: Uhhh...Did you just put me on the same level as an insect...?

Y-KO: Hmm, good point. Calling me a Venus Sebas trap is putting me down.

ME: No, me! **It's putting me down!**

Y-KO: ...Okay, how about this, then?

ME: ...?

Y-KO: You can't stop; you can't quit. Sebas crackers!

ME: That would mean you're the one who can't get away...

And if either of us is truly trapped here, it's me.
I don't think I'll ever get away from Y-ko.
She's got me firmly trapped in her clutches.

You can't stop; you can't quit.

...It's not too bad, actually.

Suit.

2006/12/23 23:07

Christmas presents.
I prefer to ask what the other person would want and then exchange the desired items on the big day.

So.

This year, for my Christmas present,
I requested what I wanted last year: a suit.
... Y-ko loves suits, too.

Y-KO:	So, about the usual suit present...
ME:	Yes?
Y-KO:	**I want to make it a surprise this year.**
ME:	...Pardon? A surprise?
Y-KO:	Yes, a surprise.

Surprise...
Which would mean, I'm assuming, that I won't know precisely what kind of suit she bought me?

ME:	...I'm sorry, but uhh... normally you have to try on a suit to make sure it's fitted properly, y'know?
Y-KO:	Of course. Nothing looks worse than an ill-fitting suit.

ME: Which would mean I have to try on the
        suit...
        ...thus ruining the element of surprise.

Y-KO: **Tsk, tsk, tsk.** How naive, Sebas.

ME: What?

D-don't tell me that she's capable of eyeballing suit sizes so
precisely, I won't even need to try it on before she buys it!

What a pointless talent that would be!
But kind of nice!

...I thought on the spot,
but once again, she forged onward by betraying my
expectations.

Y-KO: This year, you should buy your own
        Christmas present suit.
        That way you can try it on yourself
        beforehand, right?

ME: ...Huh?

I'd pick out my own present?
True, that would eliminate any problems with the fit...
...but where's the surprise in that?

ME: **I have to pick out my own
        suit?**

Y-KO: That's right. You'd better settle on a sharp
        one!

ME: ...Me picking out my own suit is a "surprise"?
Y-KO: That's right.

...Uh.

...Okay.

So that's your plan, Y-ko.

Y-KO: So, I won't have any idea what kind of suit you bought until Christmas day!

I'm so excited to find out what sort of suit you'll wear!

ME: ....

...Yes.

— True, it is a surprise.

Your entire idea is a surprise!

Y-KO: And if you make sure to bring home a suit that I like, there'll be a reward in it for you.

ME: ...A reward?

Y-KO: Yes! I will reward you by stepping on you!

ME: How is that in any way a reward?!

What a creepy sexual turn-on!
Sorry, Y-ko, but I don't roll that way!

Y-KO: Oh, sorry. Good point.

ME: Well, as long as you get it right...

Y-KO: I'll make sure to step on you with my high heels!

ME: Never mind, you've got it completely wrong!

What do you mean "make sure"?
You act as though that was the missing ingredient!

ME: Look, maybe you're under a mistaken impression...I'm not a total masochist, babe!

You know that, right?! If anything — — **I'm a slight masochist!**

I definitely don't derive any pleasure from being stepped on!
......Right?...Yeah, right. I think.
I mean, I'm only a *slight* masochist. Just a slight one.

Y-KO:	......
ME:	......
Y-KO:	......
ME:	......Would you stop giving me that cold, disgusted glare?
Y-KO:	Sorry, not gonna happen.
ME:	...Please?
Y-KO:	What about the suit?
ME:	...I'll buy it on my own.
Y-KO:	Very good. I am expecting a gorgeous one, Sebas.
ME:	Yes, ma'am. I'm looking forward to it, too. I like picking out clothes.
Y-KO:	And you like being stepped on, too.
ME:	What's with your obsession with stepping on me?!
Y-KO:	It's a desire that stems from intellectual curiosity.
ME:	How is that in any way intellectual?!

It's a curiosity without the least shred of intellect involved!

Y-KO:	Or wait, maybe I'm thinking of ineffectual curiosity.
ME:	That sounds like something you're better off without.

Y-KO: **As they say, curiosity killed the Sebas.**

ME: Why am I the one who dies?!

Y-KO: **The cause: death by moe.**

ME: ......!

I hate the fact that I thought "**that wouldn't be so bad**" for just an instant!

Y-KO: Death by moe trampling?

ME: What's with the fixation with stepping on me?! Plus, not only do I not find being stepped on "moe," it also won't kill me!

Y-KO: What if I wore my heels?

ME: How did you get this belief that I love high heels so much?!

Y-KO: Because I want shoes for my present this year. Ones with nice high heels.

ME: ......I see.

Y-KO: So let's go buy some tomorrow.

ME: ...All right.

That sure was a roundabout way to get to the point... So roundabout, it doesn't even qualify as *roundabout*?
...Oh, whatever.

Sometimes I wish she would just come out and tell me what she wants without all the joking...

Merry Christmas, everyone.

Christmas.

So.
This year's Christmas.
As my girlfriend wished, she got her shoes.

On the other hand...
I went out and bought a suit Y-ko would like.
And remember, this is supposed to be my Christmas present we're talking about.

Oh well, it's not a big deal.

...A suit Y-ko would like.
This is a surprisingly difficult choice to make.

I'm a student, but I already own several suits.
I got most of them for the purpose of working part-time jobs, and Y-ko really seems to get a kick out of them, which is great, but...

Here comes another suit.

...Even Y-ko can't wind up being completely thrilled when I end up bringing home another example of the same old thing.
So my plan is simple.
First, run through the items I already have.

Striped? Check.
Black? Check.
Gray? Check.

...I've got two buttons, three buttons, and even three buttons extending to the reverse of the flap.

...Huh?

Seems to me like I've got all the bases covered...

That means we have a problem.

No matter what I buy, I'll have something resembling it in my closet already, which means any excitement Y-ko derives from the suit will be minimal.

That's not a good thing.
That's a very bad thing.

I even considered going the distance and buying a formal tuxedo.

But...

There's hardly any call for a student to need a tuxedo.
Even if it does make Y-ko happy,
I have to admit that I hesitate at the thought of dropping a month's worth of living expenses on an outfit simply for Y-ko's sake.

So...
...What do I do?

As I wandered around the men's garments area, mulling over my options,
I saw a term flash into the corner of my eye.

It was...

Three-piece suit.

...Yes.
The combination of a jacket and pants with...

...a vest added to the mix.

Yep.

Could this be the very thing that would capture Y-ko's heart over any other option?
My choice was made...

December 24, Christmas eve.
At our prearranged meeting spot.

Y-KO:	Thanks for waiting...not long, I hope?
ME:	No, it's fine.
	...Oh, like I promised, I'm wearing the new suit.

Y-KO:	Just what I've been waiting for…except for the coat that completely covers it!
ME:	Sorry, you'll just have to wait.
Y-KO:	Take that thing off.
ME:	It's too cold!
Y-KO:	I'm only kidding…but based on what I can see of your legs, it seems like a pretty normal outfit.
ME:	I suppose.
Y-KO:	It would have been funny to see you in an all-white suit or something.
ME:	…You want me to make a significant investment for the sake of being funny? Plus, this is a Christmas present, so it's your money I'm talking about, you know?
Y-KO:	You've got a point. Let me rephrase that. **It would have been moe to see you in an all-white suit.**
ME:	…A significant investment for the sake of being moe?
Y-KO:	**I'd be prepared to throw a few hundred thousand yen down for that.**
ME:	No hesitation with that answer, huh…

Okay, so I knew to expect that…

I mean, every time I try to work a figure out of her for how much she's spent on manga and dōjinshi over the years, the most I can get is a smile and an "I don't even want to think about it."

Not that she'd regret even a bit of it, regardless of how big that number was.
... I'm almost a bit jealous of the way she lives.
There's nothing in my life that I can feel that enthusiastic about...

Y-KO: Well, whatever. Let's get going.
ME: ...Okay.

As we went to the dessert shop for the Christmas cake I had ordered,
I made sure to liberally compliment her on her new shoes,
and then we headed back to Y-ko's house.

Thirty minutes later.

ME: Well, here we are.
Y-KO: ...**Now get that coat off, Sebas,** and let me have a good look at the suit you picked out!
ME: ...Well, all right...

I slowly unfastened the coat buttons.
Removed the article that had been covering the upper half of my suit all evening.
It's showtime.

ME: ...Ta-daa!
Y-KO: What? It looks just like any old ——**?!**

She stopped moving.
There was silence.

ME:	......
Y-KO:	......
ME:	......
Y-KO:	**Mr. Sebas.**
ME:	Yes?
Y-KO:	What is that I can see peeking out from between your jacket and your shirt?
ME:	Why, that is what we call a vest.
Y-KO:	A vest, you say?
ME:	Correct.
Y-KO:	Meaning, beneath that jacket you are wearing another sleeveless suit.

...Sleeveless suit?

ME:	Well... Yes, I suppose you could describe it that way.
Y-KO:	**...Sebas!**
ME:	Yes?
Y-KO:	**I will stomp you to your heart's content tonight!**
ME:	What kind of punishment is that!?
Y-KO:	**It's a reward, not a punishment!**
ME:	If you want to reward me, think of something else!
Y-KO:	And I'm not going to skimp out on you with heels! I'll go with full boots, my darling!

ME: That can only result in broken bones.

Y-KO: Oh, don't worry! The boots are cushioned, so I'll have plenty of support!

ME: Not yours! I'm talking about my bones!
           If you stomp on me with boots, you're going to crack my bones right in two!

Y-KO: Oh, shut up about that already!
            Look — —

Just take it off.

ME: B-but what about the cake?

Y-KO: The cake doesn't matter! Take that jacket off!
            Once it's off, I'd damn well better see an outfit that a real Sebastian would wear!
            Hurry, hurry — **take it off!**

…!

Y-ko's eyes are glinting with intent!

Y-KO: **— Oh, never mind.**

ME: …Huh?

…?

Wh-what?

Have I just been spared?

ME: Umm…**I don't have to take it off now?**

Y-KO: Correct. I've got a better plan.

Y-KO: **Ahh...Merry Christmas, me!!**

ME: Well, I'm glad you're happy...

Y-KO: I'm glad to be alive!!

ME: Uhh...cool...

Oh dear...
Her eyes are glittering and sparkling...

— She's going to be so disappointed...

Once she learns that the back of this vest...

...is just plain lining.

That's right.

The vest looks crisp and smart when viewed from the front.

But viewed from behind, it's like this.

...Alas.

She'll probably be furious...even though it's not my fault.

If you have a problem with this, take it up with the gentlemen in England...

...I thought silently
as I pulled the jacket off.

Y-KO:	Eh-heh-heh...That's right...Let's see that... vest...
ME:	......
Y-KO:	......
ME:	......
Y-KO:	**What's with the back...?**
ME:	...It's sort of like lining...but that's how they come.
Y-KO:	**Why?**
ME:	Because if the back was of the normal suit material, you'd get extremely muggy with the jacket on top like I just had.

Also, it's not considered normal protocol to wear just the vest without the jacket.

After all, the gentlemen in England who developed the three-piece suit could never have guessed that there would be people in Japan who would find the vest itself to be **"moe."**

Y-KO:	**...Yes, I see...So that's why it's plain lining...**
ME:	...Y-ko...

Her eyes...They're dead inside...
Well, she was *really* excited over the whole thing...

ME:	Please cheer up...If there's anything I can do, just say the word.
Y-KO:	.........Anything...?
ME:	Yes. Well, keeping in mind that there are things I can and cannot do...
Y-KO:	...All right. Why don't you get down on all fours over there?
ME:	Down on all fours...?
Y-KO:	And then wait. I'll get the heels and boots.
ME:	What? What are you going to do?!
Y-KO:	**Stomp on you.**
ME:	I thought that was supposed to be a reward!
Y-KO:	Nope. I've changed my mind. If I had to call it something, it'd be — —

misguided rage?

ME:　　　Please, no!

And why am I getting in trouble for buying a three-piece suit just to make her happy?!

Silly Chat From a Silly Couple.

2006/12/29 21:10

So, I realize this story is full of flirting
(in fact, the entire thing may well consist of nothing but us flirting),
but on this update, likely the last for this calendar year,
I will unleash a storm of frivolous chat the scale of
which has never been seen here before.

So, for your reading pleasure,
a morning conversation between me and Y-ko on a day off.

Beep, beep, beep, beep, beep...
I woke up with the usual alarm.

I slowly withdrew my arm from beneath Y-ko's head and
slipped out of the bed.

Y-KO: ...Mmm...morning...?
ME: Yep, it's morning.
Y-KO: Ugh, I'm still so sleepy...
               ...Doesn't the old childhood friend
               usually wake up the protagonist
               in the morning?

She mumbled from the bed,
"...Kinda sudden, don't you think?
The childhood friend coming over to wake you up in the
morning...
True, it's an all-too-common pattern in stories."

ME: ...Yeah, I guess that would be the cliché.
Y-KO: Want to try it out?
ME: Try it...?

As seen often in manga, the female friend comes over to
wake up her male classmate and pal.
You want us to try out (?) this scene...

In what way would Y-ko wake me up that fits under this
mold?
Could be interesting.

Y-KO: **I'm going back to sleep, so come back in ten minutes and wake me up like a good friend would.**

ME: **I have to wake you up?!**

Wouldn't *I* normally be the protagonist under these circumstances?

Y-KO: Yeah, you got it. Thanks.

ME: ...All right...Sure thing. Back in another ten minutes?

Y-KO: Thanks, **old pal Sebas**...yawn...

And she closed her eyes again.
...Damn! And I love going back to sleep...

...What if she just did this so she could have an excuse to fall back asleep?

Oh well.
Anyway, waking someone up as if you were their best friend...
How to go about doing this?

...Should I wear my school uniform...?
Well, it's certainly cold enough to justify that.

Ten minutes later,
I was dressed in my button-up high school uniform.

Without any better ideas for how to make this more childhood friendish, I headed toward Y-ko in the bed.

...No really, how should I do this?

I started by sitting at the edge of the bed.
Y-ko always sleeps facing to her right, so of course I sat down facing her directly.

...And she looked so blissfully happy, sleeping there...

I tried caressing her hair.

...No response.

I leaned over and kissed her cheek.

...No response.

ME: **Y-ko —**

No response.
Y-ko just lay there, eyes closed, breathing slowly.

I continued talking, unperturbed.

ME: **— I love you.**

......Silence.

...For an instant, she stopped breathing.

...She's awake, isn't she?
You don't just drop dead asleep like that, ten minutes after being awake.

ME:	......
Y-KO:	......
ME:	......Should I say it again?
Y-KO:	...No, I heard you.
ME:	**I love you, Y-ko.**
Y-KO:	...I know that.
ME:	Good morning.
Y-KO:	Morning.
ME:	...Was that properly in character?
Y-KO:	What kind of childhood friend strokes your hair, kisses you, and says he loves you?!
ME:	Well, I am wearing my uniform.
Y-KO:	That's not the point!
ME:	Okay, I'll make a note of it.
Y-KO:	**Start over from elementary school!** **And make sure you read a lot more manga back then!**
ME:	Actually, I wore this style of uniform in elementary school, too.
Y-KO:	**Wha —?!** I don't know why that's supposed to be a comeback, but it sounds really cute!

...Anyway.
She's up and awake now.

ME:　　　　　You'll probably want to get into your clothes before you catch a fever.

Those pajamas are pretty sheer.

Y-KO:　　　　Hmm, good idea.

She plodded out of bed.
Even with the heater warming up the room, it felt cold.
She shivered visibly.

Y-KO:　　　　Brr, it's so cold...What's for breakfast?
ME:　　　　　Laputa toast and boob-growing juice.

* Laputa toast: Toast topped with an egg sunny-side up, as eaten by Pazu and Sheeta in a scene in *Laputa: Castle in the Sky*. Gobbling up the egg first and eating the toast second is also highly recommended!

Y-KO:　　　　Okay, I'll take a shower first.
　　　　　　　Just be ready; don't cook it yet. I want it as fresh as possible.
ME:　　　　　Got it.

She headed for the bathroom.
I headed for the kitchen.

But for some reason, she stopped and turned around.

Y-KO: ...Hey.
ME: Yes?
Y-KO: ......I love you, too.
ME: ...I know.
Y-KO: Oh. Fine, then.
ME: Yep.

I stood in the kitchen still in my uniform.

...So.
Where to go on today's date...?

As I mulled it over,
I got out the soy milk and started cutting fruit, making
preparations for the breast-augmenting elixir.

Thirty minutes later...
Clack went the door of the bathroom.

Y-KO: Heh-heh-heh...
ME: Are you finally...done...?

I turned around,
took in what Y-ko was wearing — and froze.

No, no, no.
Why?

Why —

Why are you wearing your school uniform?!

Okay, yeah, I realize I'm wearing mine, but still —!

What makes you think I want to go out on a date in my high school uniform at this age?!

Y-KO: Oh, come on! You're wearing yours!

ME: Then I'm taking it off...

Y-KO: No, I want to take it off you!

ME: ...Then I want to take yours off you.

Y-KO: Go right ahead.

ME: How shameless! **That's the part where you act modestly!**

...Sigh.

Get ready for another long year of being manipulated...

...Am I going to put up with this forever?

Sometimes I wish I could have the upper hand with her.
After all, as soon as the New Year starts —

I'm taking her to meet my parents.

Taking My Girlfriend to Meet My Parents.

2007/01/02 18:40

Happy New Year's everyone.

So.
Let's get started with the first update of the year.
It'll be shorter than usual, but such is life.

My parents are currently living in America due to their work situation.
The transfer came out of the blue last summer,
but they've grown used to life over there in the meantime,
and it sounds like they're quite enjoying themselves.

Last fall,
I received an e-mail from my father.

SUBJECT:	Re:
BODY:	**I'd like to meet your girlfriend sometime.**
	You should bring her here over the holidays.
	We'll put up the travel expenses, of course.
	Dad

ME:	......

I froze, message open.

...Well, all right, I did have an inkling that this might happen sooner or later.

...But this is a little too far on the "sooner" side, Dad.

I turned around and called out to Y-ko, who was organizing materials on her laptop.

ME:	Can I ask you something, Y-ko?
Y-KO:	Sure. What's up?

ME: My parents are asking me to introduce you to them over the New Year.

Y-KO: ...Me? Meet them?

ME: That's right.

Y-KO: ...Aren't your parents in America right now?

ME: Well, yes.

Y-KO: ......Umm.

ME: ......?

Y-KO: There's one big problem.

ME: Yes?

Y-KO: **I don't know if I can introduce myself in English!**

ME: ....Huh?

— Do I really want to go through with this?

Taking My Girlfriend to Meet My Parents, Part 2.

At the end of the year.
At a time when a certain major dōjinshi event was being held in a certain convention center.

I was nowhere to be found at that center; I was at the airport.

— Taking my girlfriend to America so that I could show her to my parents.

Y-KO: **...Sightosheeingu...for four deizu...**

Y-ko stood at my side, nervously clutching her passport.
As this was her first trip out of the country, she was slightly spooked about the ordeal.

...To be honest,

I felt much the same way on my first trip overseas,
so I could understand her anxiety.

ME: ...There's still a bit of time to kill...Want to
               check out the duty-free shops?
Y-KO: Hmm? Sure. Actually, what I'd really like to do
               is master the sentences I need to rattle off in
               order to get through immigration!

Y-ko stared fiercely at the sample statements she had
printed up from the Internet.
Aww, isn't that cute?

Actually, it seems like she's more nervous about the immigra-
tion check upon landing than about meeting my parents...

Well, I understand how she feels.
Plus, it's not like she has anything to be anxious about with
my folks.

Y-KO: ...Hey! What are you smirking about?!
ME: I'm trying to burn this scene into my memory,
               because I've never seen you so nervous
               about anything before.
Y-KO: Oh, yuck! You are such a creep!
ME: It'll be fine.
Y-KO: Thanks for the consolation!
ME: Plus, if they have to interrogate us in separate
               rooms, you do have the right to request an
               interpreter.

Y-KO: Okay, never mind, that sounds more like a
          threat than a consolation!

Ooh, what a glare.
...In fact, I might be forgiven for thinking it was a dead
serious glare.

Two hours later.

We filed into an airplane with an American airline company's
name painted in gaudy colors on its outside and searched
through the spacious cabin for our seats.
...Ah, there they are.
Yes, good old economy class.
Compact? Cozy? Let's call it out for what it is — cramped.

Y-KO: Is this it? Oh, wow...All the people here are
          Americans.
ME: Makes sense. They probably want to spend
          the holidays at home.

We stored our bags in the overhead bins and sat down.

Y-KO: ...Why couldn't your parents come back to
          Japan for the holidays instead?
ME: Well, it's too late for that now...
          Hey, are you feeling okay? You don't look so
          good.
Y-KO: ...Okay, I didn't tell you this before...but this
          is my first time on an airplane!

ME: What?! Really?!

Y-KO: I think I'm a little freaked out about this...

ME: I can see why... But you'll be fine once we get in the air.

Y-KO: ...W-will you hold my hand?

ME: ...Huh? Well, sure, I don't mind...

Baby, when you hesitantly ask me to do something like that, well...
It gives me a nervous thrill completely different from the kind you usually send running down my spine.

— I felt a squeeze.
She had grabbed my left hand.

Y-KO: ...If we fall and crash, I'll step on you until the moment we die!

ME: Not only is that a terrible thing to think about, we'll die before you have time to step on me.

Y-KO: Then I'll step on you before we crash.

ME: Why?!

Y-KO: Stress release. Take that!

ME: Ouch!

This is so unfair!
Plus, that was so not a "step"! That was a kick!
Not to mention, how did it take me this long to realize that she really likes stomping on me?

Y-KO: There, I'm feeling a bit better now.

ME: ...It was worth being stomped on.

Y-KO: You know what? Next time you should get some bumpy warts installed on your foot.

ME: Why? So you can release stress and get a foot massage at the same time?!

Y-KO: You know, you have a really weird and lame ability to shout in a low voice.

ME: Don't call it lame!

Y-KO: Fine, it's spectacularly lame.

ME: That just makes it sound worse!

Suddenly, an announcement in English rang through the cabin,
drowning out our silly bickering.
Looks like the flight is about to begin.

At my side, Y-ko affixed her seat belt, looking determined and serious.
...A little too grave, my dear.
I understand how you're feeling, though.

The voice in English spoke up again, announcing the expected arrival time.

ME: ......

Y-KO: ......

ME: ......

Y-KO: ......I can't tell what he's saying...

ME: Well, that's no surprise.

Y-KO: ......Translate for me...

...Whoa.

This time she pleaded with tears in her eyes.
...It was such a rare sight, I felt a tug at my
heart.

Y-KO: Please? Will you? All the staff are Americans,
               so I have no one else to rely on...

Wow!
Y-ko acting honest and straightforward for once!
What's gotten into her?

Y-KO: Please?...Please.
ME: Well, sure...But you know they'll
               announce the same thing in Japanese
               next, right?
Y-KO: ......
ME: ......
Y-KO: ......**Huh?**
ME: They have a Japanese announcement,
               too.
Y-KO: ...Wh-what? They're **also** going to tell us
               the same stuff in Japanese?
ME: Well, sure. The flight's leaving from Japan.
               Of course they're going to announce that
               stuff for us.
Y-KO: ......

ME: Oh, and by the way, they'll always have a flight attendant who can speak Japanese.

Y-KO: Really?!

ME: Why would I lie about that?

Y-KO: ...Sheesh! There's nothing to be afraid of, then!

ME: There isn't?

Y-KO: Yeah, I'll be completely fine!

ME: So I don't have to hold your hand anymore?

Y-KO: **...Actually, you do.**

ME: **.........Pardon?**

Y-KO: ...This engine noise is kind of scaring me, so I don't want to let go.

ME: ......That's very honest of you.

Y-KO: Good. I was worried you might refuse to hold my hand anymore.

...Aww, hell!
Why does she keep acting so timid and helpless?!

**It's so different from normal!
I don't get it, but it sure is cute!**

...I thought, as the plane sped up.

And then,
the moment of liftoff.

Y-KO:　　　　　　**......!**

— Squeeze.

The pressure on my left hand grew even firmer.
...Come on.

— Really, what's the big deal?

Are you trying to moe me to death?

Taking My Girlfriend to Meet My Parents, Part 3.

`2007/01/12 22:55`

After ten-plus hours in an airplane,
the craft touched down safely in an international airport
within America.

After passing through customs (Y-ko having survived the
process handily),
we walked to the lobby, where we would meet my parents.
As they weren't there yet, we sat on a bench to wait.

Either out of relief at making it through the customs gauntlet
unscathed
or trepidation at the imminent meeting with my parents —

Y-ko was slightly more wound up than usual.

Y-KO: Oh, crap! We're in New York! Starting today,
               I'm a New Yorker!

ME:	Well, I can certainly tell you you're not a New Yorker.
Y-KO:	Who cares? It's a mental thing!
ME:	A mental thing?
Y-KO:	Plus, remember how I was able to speak English properly?
ME:	...You were?
Y-KO:	Yes. I told the flight attendant I wanted "pasta, please." The fact that I was able to communicate with a foreigner means I'm a New Yorker now!
ME:	Sounds like the bar has been set pretty low...
Y-KO:	But when she said, "Something or pasta," I couldn't make out what the other word was, so I just ended up going with pasta.
ME:	You don't make much of a New Yorker!
Y-KO:	Bah. So what? I'm a Tokyoite to the core.
ME:	That's the first I've heard of it!
Y-KO:	I'm a true-blue child of Tokyo.
ME:	...When you eat soba noodles, how much do you dip them in the broth?
Y-KO:	Not at all, actually.
ME:	Wow, you are a Tokyoite!

The stereotype is that people from Tokyo don't like to use much broth with their soba!

Y-KO:	Plus, I don't think you're **so bad** yourself.
ME:	...Thanks. Thanks a lot.

Now we're moving on to puns?
The sentiment is appreciated, however.

Y-KO:	In fact, that soba you made with yam was incredible.
ME:	Thank you!

Wait, now it's not a pun?
This is so embarrassing! This conversation is driving me crazy!

Y-KO:	Really, it was awesome.
ME:	Great...
Y-KO:	How'd you make the broth?
ME:	Five parts water to each part stock!

It was your ordinary bottled broth from the store!
In fact, so were the noodles! The entire thing was bought at the grocery store,
which would mean that my preparation had **absolutely no effect on the taste!**

Y-KO:	I see. So that's your secret ingredient, huh?
ME:	Which part, the water or the stock?
Y-KO:	**The stock.**
ME:	Using **preprepared stock** kind of negates the entire concept of a secret ingredient.

How is any of that "secret"?

It's all coming from a bottle of seaweed noodle broth.
Thanks, Yamasa Corporation, for your fine line of soy
sauce–based products!

As our usual frivolous repartee carried on,
I received a call on my phone.

... It's from Dad.
Beep —

ME:	Hello?
DAD:	Aha! Did you land all right? We're about to reach the airport. Where are you?
ME:	Uhh, we're sitting on a bench in front of the car rental counter.
DAD:	Okay, great. We'll be there in another five minutes.
ME:	Got it. See you then.

Beep —
Conversation over.

ME:	They'll be here in five minutes.
Y-KO:	... Okay. Getting nervous now.

... Aha.
She's nervous; she's nervous!
It's nice to see this side of her for once.

Y-KO: ...You can't help but get shaky nerves once this moment comes around.

ME: Ha-ha. See how I felt last year?

Y-KO: Yeah. It was a lot of fun seeing you freak out, though.

ME: And now the tables are turned.

Y-KO: I guess they are.

ME: I'm sure you'll get used to my parents right away, though.
               They're the kind of people who can open up to strangers immediately.

Y-KO: But still, it won't change the fact that I'm nervous...

ME: Ha-ha, just be yourself.

Y-KO: Myself...?

ME: That's right. Be who you really are. The usual one I see all the time...

Y-KO: ......The usual me?

ME: ......The usual you...

Our eyes met.

Yes.
My geeky, **fujoshi girlfriend.**

Y-KO: ....Are you sure that's a good idea?

...Well, at least she's aware that it could be considered a problem.

Of course, she wouldn't be a **secret fujoshi** if she wasn't aware of that.

ME:	.........Really, I think you can afford to be the usual Y-ko.
Y-KO:	I can?
ME:	Wouldn't you get exhausted trying to pretend to be someone else all the time?
Y-KO:	Well, yeah, but...
ME:	I'm not saying you should force your otaku nature out into the open,
	but you should not have to force it into the **closet**, either.

Yep.
It's going to be a monumentally draining task to hide something like that your whole life.
She ought to take some of the weight off her shoulders.

ME:	Plus, my parents are fans of manga.
Y-KO:	Really?! Wow, I'm feeling closer to them already.
ME:	In fact, they gave me an entire manga set for a Christmas present one year.
Y-KO:	You never told me that.
ME:	Man, that takes me back...Had the whole series lined up on the shelf.
Y-KO:	Which one?
ME:	A *History of Japan* manga series.

Y-KO:	That's what I figured! Good thing I didn't get my hopes up.
ME:	Okay, enough of the jokes.

Here we go.
I stood up and grabbed my luggage.
Pointed my finger at a couple that had just entered the lobby.

ME:	My parents are here.
Y-KO:	......
ME:	C'mon, let's go.

Y-ko and I started walking toward them.
They seemed to have spotted us as they were now walking in our direction.

ME:	Still nervous?
Y-KO:	Can't you tell? I'm stiff as a board.
ME:	Ha-ha, you can play it natural. It's not like you're coming here **to ask for their daughter's hand in marriage**.
Y-KO:	Good point. If anything, I'm **asking for their son** instead.
ME:	I can't imagine a moment in this trip when that will be necessary.
Y-KO:	Right now!
ME:	Umm...Are you sure you're really feeling nervous...?

Y-KO:	Hey, you were the one who told me to act natural.
ME:	I figured there would be some kind of limit to that.

Who is she kidding? She's cool as a cucumber right now.
And then we arrived at my parents' side.
. . . It's been quite a while since I saw them, as a matter of fact.

ME:	Well . . . Long time no see. Have you been good?
DAD:	Yep.
MOM:	Yes.
ME:	. . . . . .

. . . Uh, excuse me?
I'm talking to you, so you could afford to throw me a glance or two.
Clearly excited, they stared straight at my girlfriend.

. . . I suppose I should do the introductions.

ME:	Uhh . . . Well, this is my father, and this is my mother.
DAD:	It's so good of you to take care of this big lug for us.
MOM:	It's nice to meet you.
ME:	And this is my girlfriend, Y-ko.

— What happened to acting like your natural self, Y-ko!? You're acting like some kind of Goody Two-shoes!

...And look at that!

I can see that look in my parents' eyes! It's that **well done, my boy!** look!

...Though thinking on it now, Y-ko's always had a talent for disguising herself as someone else.

This is probably small beans to her!

Taking My Girlfriend to Meet My Parents, Part 4.

2007/01/21 20:13

Inside a car speeding down the highway.
Y-ko murmured in the backseat.

...A suddenly demure Y-ko, *murmuring*.

Y-KO:	...It's so peaceful out here.
DAD:	People think New York's entirely urban, but it's only the city.

My father answered from the driver's seat.
Wherever it is my parents live,
it's not smack in the middle of the big city.

ME:	It tells you a lot about my dad that he claims to be on assignment in New York.
DAD:	Well, it's not a lie.

ME: Can I please have the admiration I felt when I
                first heard the big news back, then?
DAD: Hey, I'm working for a small enterprise, son.
                Things like that don't happen to just anyone.
ME: Why do you sound proud of that?

The first conversation since our grand reunion, and I'm
already depressed.
My mother, sitting in the passenger seat, turned to Y-ko.

MOM: You were probably hoping for big things
                when you heard New York, weren't you?
Y-KO: Oh no. He told me what kind of place this
                was, so it's pretty much what I'd expected.
MOM: It is? Well, good. You'll probably find it boring,
                but I hope it's at least comfortable.
Y-KO: Thank you very much. Plus, this is my first
                trip overseas.
                Even this scenery is fresh and exciting to me.
MOM: Really? I'm glad to hear that.
                ...Ah, we're almost there. It's been a long trip
                for you, hasn't it?
Y-KO: Not too bad. Tiring, but even more enjoyable.

...Hmm.
She's got this disguise down perfectly.
The whole time, I was enjoying the conversation,
wondering when she would slip up.
Well, I suppose she spends every day wearing the
uniform of an office lady...

My poor parents have no idea...

We arrived at the house, and Y-ko and I put our luggage in the guest room, where we would be staying.
My parents went out immediately to Walmart to do some shopping.

We sat on the couch and took a breather.

Y-KO:	Man, I'm tired...
ME:	It must be tiring to play a role so seamlessly...
Y-KO:	...? No, it's just from the flight and car ride.
ME:	Huh? You're not tired from pretending to be someone else? You certainly have my parents fooled...
Y-KO:	Oh, please. Are you calling that some kind of devious act? I'm only showing them the face I always wear.
ME:	...Always?
Y-KO:	**When you rip off the fujoshi mask, the OL face is exposed.**
ME:	Oh, so it was me who you've been fooling all along!

And this whole time, I thought the fujoshi bit was her real personality!

Y-KO:	...Hmm, you seem to be speaking a bit differently than usual.

ME: I am?

Y-KO: I don't know. You typically don't act this aggressive with me.

ME: ...Uh...well...Maybe I just find it weird to act so polite around my parents.

Y-KO: And that's why you're acting different.

ME: ...Do you find it weird?

Y-KO: Actually, it's kind of hot. You sound like a tsundere.

ME: Okay, never mind. I will be as polite and demure as always!

Is that all it takes to make someone a tsundere?!
I'd better watch how I act from now on if I don't want to
be tainted by that word!

Y-KO: Okay, the tsundere part was a joke...but I don't mind, really. You can act that way around your parents.

ME: Really? You don't mind?

Y-KO: I'm going to step on you later, though.

ME: Rather a disagreeable exchange, I think...

Y-KO: I'll give you a nice flat nose.

ME: Nose?! You're going to stomp on my face?!

Y-KO: Well, it would be a shame to sterilize you at such a young age.

ME: My face and my crotch are the only options?

Y-KO: It's an equal exchange.

ME: Your rates are a bit outrageous, madam!

Y-KO:	Well, I've inherited the spirit of the unequal treaties.
ME:	At least you're honest about it.
Y-KO:	**Open your nation's borders to us.** Did I sound like him?
ME:	Sound like who?
Y-KO:	Commodore Perry.
ME:	I have no way to tell, but if I had to guess, I'd say you didn't!

Unfortunately, I don't know Perry personally, so I can't say for sure!
Plus, since when was Perry associated with the unequal treaties?

Y-KO:	**Pleez give me your son!**
ME:	Sorry, no can do.
Y-KO:	**HA-HA-HA! Thees must be thee famous Japaneez tsundere!**
ME:	Wow, Perry knows a lot about Japanese culture...And since when was that tsundere?
Y-KO:	**I lub you forever. You are tsundere!**
ME:	So Commodore Perry has fallen in love with me...madly and eternally...and declared me to be a tsundere?!
Y-KO:	...Adulterer!
ME:	And now I've been labeled an adulterer despite never requiting his feelings. Great.
Y-KO:	I'll tell your parents.
ME:	Tell them what?

That their son was labeled a tsundere and then propositioned by Commodore Perry?
Okay, true, that might thrust my personal reputation into a minor crisis…

Y-KO: To give me their son.

ME: That's a request, not a revelation.

Y-KO: I have taken your son alive.

ME: Sorry, we don't have enough money to meet your hostage demands.

Y-KO: Your son has been in a terrible accident. Please send emergency funds to…

ME: And now you're running a scam!

Y-KO: **If anything, your son is on the uke side of the equation.**

ME: That could drive our family completely dysfunctional!

Y-KO: And he's a total masochist.

ME: I'm not a total masochist! I'm a **slight masochist!**

How many times must I explain that?
That's the kind of place where a man has to take a stand and stick up for himself!

Y-KO: Wow, you're really in a feisty mood today. The comebacks are about to give me whiplash. Have you been possessed by the spirit of Mimura?

* Comedian of the comedy duo Summers.

ME: No idea what Mimura has to do with any of
              this, but...
              ...I think the less sleep I've had, the crankier
              I get.
Y-KO: Oh, I know what you mean...Are you sleepy?
ME: ...Do you mind if I take a little nap?
              I don't think they'll be back for a little while
              longer.
Y-KO: Want me to take my clothes off?
ME: I'll live, thanks.

**Where did that one come from?
Why would you need to strip?**

Y-KO: I just thought maybe you'd like to use my
              legs as a pillow for once.
ME: ....There's nothing that says it has to be
              your bare legs.
Y-KO: Really? Fine, then...Come and get your
              jeans pillow, **big boy**.

...Well, if you insist.
I didn't get any sleep on the flight, after all...

Plop.

ME: ...Good night.
Y-KO: Good night.

— And then...

...Hmm?
...Oh, I fell asleep.

Y-ko...?
...Huh? The leg pillow has turned into a regular pillow...

......

......I can hear voices.
Excited, laughing voices...

Dad...Mom...and Y-ko's voices...

— Oh no!

■ ■ ■ ■ ■

......What time is it now?

IT'S NOW TWO HOURS LATER... AND I HEAR MY PARENTS AND Y-KO CHATTING FROM THE LIVING ROOM...

I slept in!
I slept way in!!

You should have woken me up, Y-ko!
I hurriedly rushed out into the living room.

DAD: Aha, you're awake.
MOM: Good morning. Have a good nap?

Good morning?!
Why didn't any of you people wake me up?!

DAD: Well, well, that was a surprise, wasn't it?
MOM: Yes, it certainly was.

…?
What are they smirking about?

Y-KO: Oh…Sorry I didn't wake you up.
DAD: No, Y-ko, you don't need to apologize for that.
MOM: Of course not. Otherwise we wouldn't have
                been treated to such a precious sight.

Precious sight…?

DAD: # I've never seen anything as

MOM: **precious as my own son fast asleep with his head on a girl's lap.**
Indeed, it was so precious, I just had to take a quick picture and e-mail it to everyone.

......
I silently stared at Y-ko.

Y-KO: Ha-ha-ha! Sorry, I guess they saw us.

... Well, uh,
how should I sum this up?

...My parents will never let me live this one down for the rest of my life.

Stupid jet lag and stupid me!
I already want to go home!!

Taking My Girlfriend to Meet My Parents, Part 5.

2007/01/28 20:40

My parents took the first shot at me.
I stood at the entrance to the living room.
...I was already reeling.

MOM:	Well, aren't you hungry? Come and eat with us.
DAD:	Probably haven't had anything but airline food, eh?
	...Your first airplane meal must have been a nasty surprise, Y-ko.
Y-KO:	But now that I've had such a wonderful meal to finish the day,
	I've forgotten all about that horrid food.
MOM:	Oh, Y-ko. You are so good at flattery!
Y-KO:	No, really! It was delicious.
	Can you give me your recipe for this fried rice later?
MOM:	Oh, this? It's easy. You just have to get the seasonings right —

......
They're hitting it off...

Y-ko is hitting it off perfectly with my parents...

DAD:	Don't just stand there like an idiot, sit down.
Y-KO:	Here, give me your cup. I'll pour you some tea.
MOM:	Oh, thank you so much, dear.
DAD:	...Do you always make her do this much work, son?

Absolutely not, Dad!
It's usually me who works this hard!

Y-KO:	No, if anyone's doing the cooking and whatnot, it's him, not me…
MOM:	Oh, don't be silly. He doesn't cause trouble, does he?
Y-KO:	No, really. He's the one who has to clean up after me all the time. Like the other day —

…Yeah, that's right!
She's telling the truth! She's telling the truth, but…

…for some reason, even though Y-ko's being absolutely honest,
my parents keep shooting me these lukewarm glances!

Dammit!!
Don't stare at me like that!

…Dad!
Were you just thinking, "She's so well mannered"?!

Why are you giving me a thumbs-up, Mom?!
…And stop mouthing "good job" at me!
…Damn!
This is supposed to be my home field (in a way),
so why do I feel such an oppressive road disadvantage?

Despite my fiercely conflicting emotions, I sat down at the table.

DAD:	By the way, Y-ko…
Y-KO:	Yes?

DAD: What was it about him, anyway?
ME: Grrfh?! Coff, gehoff!

Come on! What are you playing at, bringing up an embarrassing topic like that?!
I could have choked on my food and died!

Y-ko decided to go out with me because she saw me putting little bookmark slips in my books!

Tell me, what kind of reaction are you planning to give when she drops that bombshell?
You're kind of enjoying this, aren't you? You can't wait for her to say it!
...Okay, Pops, let's see how you uphold your fatherly image after this one!

Y-KO: Well, let's see...
...He's very nice, and sometimes he does and says things that just electrify me...
DAD: ......
MOM: ......
ME: ......

...What a difficult statement to give a reaction to!
Plus, I thought it was the slips that clinched it for me, Y-ko!

DAD: Well, er...I hope you'll keep giving him lots of love.

MOM:　　　　　Yes, please be good to our boy, Y-ko.

See? Now you made things all weird!
And for some reason, I'm feeling a bit uncomfortable!

Y-KO:　　　　Oh no. I can only hope that you will accept
　　　　　　　me.

...Ah!
I-I feel like I need to divert the course of this conversation!
I sense danger ahead!
We're moving in the wrong direction!

ME:　　　　　Oh, that reminds me. Umm, you know...
MOM:　　　　　So, Y-ko...
ME:　　　　　Oh yeah! Th-this rice is really good; it reminds
　　　　　　　me of —
MOM:　　　　　Which one of you asked the other out?
ME:　　　　　The rice is...
DAD:　　　　　Oh, I'm curious about that, too. Who popped
　　　　　　　the question, son?

No!
Listen to me!
I'm trying to describe how good the rice is!

Y-KO:　　　　Well, uh...It's actually...kind of an
　　　　　　　embarrassing topic.
　　　　　　　But it is important to us, so I'd like to keep it
　　　　　　　a secret...if you don't mind.

Thatta girl, Y-ko!
A real grown woman sure knows how to be awesome!

MOM: Don't you want to see some childhood photo albums of him?

DAD: I bet you'd love to hear all kinds of juicy, embarrassing stories.

ME: What are you people doing...?

Come on, Mom and Dad...
You're too old to act like this. Take a page out of Y-ko's book, and —

Y-KO: Well, it was a really beautiful situation.
The moon was out, and it was full and bright.
He and I had just —

ME: Y-ko?!

And now she goes ahead and spills the beans!
I hate grown-ups!

DAD: Aha, so he was the one who asked you out first?
So tell me, son. You spent about a week writing those lines, didn't you?

MOM: And then you practiced them on your own, right?

Y-KO: Huh? You did?

ME: ......!

...Yeah, so I did!
I practiced them constantly, and I had the whole situation planned out ten days in advance!
I had several patterns memorized based on different possible answers from Y-ko!

...Is there something wrong with that, dammit?!

Y-KO: Well, can you tell me about him as a little boy?

DAD: What do you want, the embarrassing anecdotes or the failures?

Stop right there, Dad!
Are those the only two choices she gets?!

DAD: Well, it's not like there are any particularly cool stories about him, right, dear?

MOM: Really? I've got some.

Look at that, Dad!
Mom understands how it works!
Tell Y-ko a really impressive tale about me as a lad, Mom!

MOM: When they asked him what he wanted to be when he grew up back in kindergarten, he made a big pose and said, **"I want to be a superhero!"**

There!
Wasn't that c-c-? Huh?!

DAD: ......

Y-KO: ......

ME: ......

MOM: Oh, but there's more —

...More?

MOM: — and I want to save Mommy from a giant monster!

.........Oh dear.

Y-KO: That's so cool!

DAD: What about me? Wasn't he going to save me, too?!

MOM: Oh, and by the way, this is a photo of him at that age —

Y-KO: Y-you have to copy me some prints of this!

MOM: Of course! I've got the negatives saved and everything!

DAD: Honey! Honey! What about me?!

..........Great.

ANOTHER ONE OF MY WEAKNESSES ADDED TO HER HAND...

SLUMP...

HEH HEH HEH...

WEAK WEAK

— Come on, Mom... Is that the only cool story about me you have to tell?

And, Y-ko, you are getting along with them much too well.

Taking My Girlfriend to Meet My Parents, Part 6.

2007/02/06 18:29

We finished dinner and returned to our room to prepare for our baths.
As soon as we got inside the room, Y-ko began laughing.

Y-KO: **Ha-ha-ha. Boy, that was a great story!** I'm glad I came!

ME: ....Well, I'm happy that you're enjoying yourself.

Y-ko was beaming full faced after hearing those stories about my childhood.
...No, wait.
This is less of a "beam" and more of a "**leer.**"

...Oh man, that is scary.

Y-KO: Well, it was funny and all...but it was also pretty endearing.

ME: Really? That lame story?

Y-KO: Yeah. I thought it was really cute.

ME: Well, that's nice...though I don't know if I should be happy about that or not.

Y-KO: From now on, I'll just have to call you **Superhero ★ Sebas**!

ME: Okay, you don't actually think it's endearing at all, do you?

She's just pulling my leg!
Plus, that's a pretty long nickname!

Y-KO: Oh, I'm kidding. But I do think it's a nice story.

ME: Well, thanks...

Y-KO: ...Come here. I'll give you a pat on the head for being a good boy.

ME:	Why?! And what exactly did I do to deserve it?
Y-KO:	I'm going to give you a pat for growing up the right way.
ME:	Rrgh...!
Y-KO:	Come on, get over here.
ME:	......

...I walked over to Y-ko's side.
The palm of her hand rubbed the top of my head.

Y-KO:	There we go. Good boy.
ME:	Ugggh...

What is this emotion? It's like embarrassment mixed with reluctance to pull away!
...Dammit! I can tell that I'm enjoying this!

I got our toiletries together for the bath and took Y-ko to the bathroom.
Since she was the guest in the house, I let her start first.

My mom showed us how to use the showerhead.
American showers work slightly differently from the ones in Japan.

MOM:	And if you press this here, it'll come out of the shower.
Y-KO:	Okay, I see. Thank you for the explanation.
MOM:	...And what are you doing here?

She looked at me with a quizzical expression.

ME: Well, I need to learn how it works, too.

Y-KO: What? You aren't coming in with me?

ME: I'm amazed that you would suggest such a thing in front of my own mom!

Y-KO: Ha-ha-ha, just kidding...Here.

...Here?

She put her arms up in the air for some reason.

ME: ...What do you want?

Y-KO: **Take my shirt off.**

ME: You are unbelievable!

What is she thinking?!
And why is Mom laughing her ass off?!

Y-KO: **As you can see, ma'am, this is how I treat him.**

MOM: Ha-ha-ha. You're right, he does act funny when you tease him.

ME: Well, okay, I can't deny that, but —

Y-KO: He's a very reliable worker, however.

MOM: What, really?

Y-KO: Yes. He's been a huge help on many occasions.

MOM: Really...**Where did we go wrong?**

ME: You went wrong?!

	Shouldn't you consider that a smashing success?!
MOM:	You could say that, too.
ME:	No, you could only say that.
MOM:	Well, I'm just not used to hearing my son paid compliments, so I didn't know how to respond.
ME:	What does this say about my reputation with you guys?!

I've been given compliments all the time!
Is this how you responded each time that happened?

MOM:	I'm sorry. You know your old mom — I'm a ditz.
ME:	The ditz excuse only works while you're still in your twenties!
Y-KO:	Really...? So I can use that and get away with it?
ME:	What are you planning to do, Y-ko?!

And then my dad appeared.

DAD:	I'm done with the wash, dear... **Whoa!** Are you taking a bath with Y-ko?

Dad...Don't make things any worse.
We've already been through this joke.

Y-KO:	Yes, we're going in together.

DAD:	**What?!**
ME:	Why would you say that, Y-ko?!
Y-KO:	…Oops, sorry. You know me, I'm just a ditz.
MOM:	And she's safe!
ME:	No she's not!
	I don't care if she's still in her twenties; it's not an automatic excuse!

And that one was clearly an out!
I'm the one who writes the rule book!

DAD:	…Is it just me, or have your put-downs been sharpened since the last time we saw you?
MOM:	They cut harder…and they have a strong flavor.
ME:	Okay, I understand the "cut"…but "flavor"? Am I a beer now?
MOM:	Fizz!
ME:	What is that, a sound effect?
DAD & MOM:	**Fizz, fizz!**
ME:	Stop harmonizing!

Oh yeah! I remember now!
For some reason, I forgot that my parents are *huge pains in the ass!*

MOM:	Oh, honey?
DAD:	Hmm? What?
MOM:	If you're done with the wash, will you wipe down the table?

DAD: Already did it.

MOM: Okay. I'll pour some drinks later if you get the glasses out.

DAD: You got it!

Hmm-hm-hm-hmmm.
Dad turned back toward the living room, humming.

...Come on, Y-ko. Don't smile like that.
I know what's going on.
I'd always had an inkling it was the case.

I just didn't want to admit it.

— The reason I can't snap back at you...

— I guess this is what they mean by, "You can't fight your nature."

Taking My Girlfriend to Meet My Parents, Part 7.

So.
The story of the face-to-face meeting of my parents and my girlfriend ends today.

My dad is driving us to the airport in his car.

The conversation naturally turns to reflect on the last few days.

DAD:	How did you like America, Y-ko?
Y-KO:	I had a lot of fun!
	It was great getting to meet you and talk to you.
MOM:	And I'm glad to hear about what this young man's been getting up to back home.
	We'll have to meet up in Japan next time.
Y-KO:	Absolutely. I'll be expecting more childhood stories, too.
	Particularly the embarrassing ones!

She still wants more...
After my poor past has already been stripped bare and savaged...

MOM: Ha-ha-ha, you can count on it.
Also, we've still got some albums left in Japan to show you.

What's with a parent's obsession with photo albums, anyway?
I've had enough of my photos being dug out of storage!

...And now Y-ko's got a whole new hand of embarrassing things she can lord over me!

MOM: Oh, and if he does anything to you, just e-mail me about it anytime you like.
Y-KO: Of course! I will!

And when did they exchange e-mail addresses?!

Plus, is it just me, or are they way too friendly?!
I mean, sure, it's better than the usual mother and daughter-in-law scenario,
but I still don't like what this relationship is implying... for me!

And Mom!

If anyone's going to get stuff done to them, chances are it's going to be me!

— And as the harmless (except to me) conversation continued, we arrived at our destination: the airport.

We put our bags on the counter, and it came time for the (exaggerated) farewells.

DAD:	Good-bye, Y-ko. You take good care of our boy.
MOM:	I hope you can overlook his many faults.
Y-KO:	Huh? Uh...okay.

Wow.
She's in serious mode for once.

DAD:	Oh, and son, be careful not to forget anything.
MOM:	And brush your teeth before you go to bed.
Y-KO:	Look left and right before you cross the signal, and raise your hand.
ME:	**Be serious! Please, treat me like a serious human being!** And why are you joining in the teasing, Y-ko?!
Y-KO:	Oh, I just thought the situation called for it. It worked out nicely, didn't it?
DAD:	But, Y-ko...**it's not the signal you cross, it's the street.**
Y-KO:	...Good point!

Yes, it may have been a good point!
But is that the best comment a father can make in this situation?!
Your son is being lectured about how to cross the street, and that's the best you can come up with?

DAD: Okay, enough of the jokes.

Ahem, he coughed.

DAD: You stay safe.
MOM: And don't forget to call.
ME: ...Right. I'll see you later.
Y-KO: Thank you for everything.
ME: Let's go.

I waved to my parents and headed through the gate with Y-ko.
...It was a short trip, but it was well worth it.

Y-KO: You've got nice, fun parents.
ME: I know, right? A bit weird, though.
Y-KO: Ha-ha-ha. But I can see why you turned out
            the way you did.
ME: Is that so?
            ...I guess that statement from you makes it
            worth the trip.
Y-KO: Plus **Papa Sebas** is a fun person.
ME: Papa Sebas?!
Y-KO: Oops, should I call him Sebas Papa?

Personally, I think Papa Sebas has a much better ring to it than Sebas Papa.

ME: **Whether Papa comes first or last is not the problem!**
My problem is with you calling my own dad Sebas!

Y-KO: Okay, got it. I'll just abbreviate Papa Sebas into Papas, then.

ME: Papas?! Are you going to kill off my dad?

Y-KO: If that happens, the question is whether I'm Bianca or Nera...
By the way, which one did you pick?

ME: No, that isn't the question... but to answer your query,
I'm the type who would prefer to play the game twice and enjoy each side of the story.

Y-KO: Aaah! I'm going to tell your mother about this!

ME: About what?!

Y-KO: Her son is an adulterer!

ME: I am no such thing!

But for some reason, I feel incredibly guilty!
Should I have picked one or the other?!

Y-KO: Heh... You will learn to rue this terrible mistake.

ME: ... Okay. Which one should I have picked?

Y-KO: Huh? Which what?

ME: Bianca or Nera? Which is the correct choice?

To be perfectly honest, if I was forced to choose one and not the other,

I'd have to go with Bianca...
I guess?

I don't really know.

Y-KO: In that case...the answer should be... **me.**
ME: ...... **What?**

...Me?

Y-KO: I don't care if they're childhood friends or rich landowners' daughters. **You are not allowed to choose any woman aside from me.** How's that?
ME: ...I get the picture.

Yes, I see.
A very bold and cool statement, especially considering it came out of a pointless discussion about video games.

...Well, damn.
Sometimes she just knows how to be cool.

......Hmm?

Wait a minute.

ME: Well, you know what that means! I can't make the jump into girl games now!
Y-KO: Huh?
ME: Well, I'm not allowed to choose any woman aside from you, right?

Even if she's from a video game.

Y-KO: ......Umm, I...guess so?

ME: Oh good! Now I don't have to worry about cheating on you with 2-D girls.
And that means you're going to stop trying to shove those games down my throat!

Yes.

She is all about the erotic games, the girl games, the dating sims.
She keeps trying to force me to play them.

Y-KO: ......Hmm...

ME: You want me to choose you, not Bianca or Nera, right?

I put the screws to her.
If I can wring a statement out of her, I win!

Y-KO: ......I guess I don't have a choice. I'll stop pushing those girl games on you.

...Victory!

I felt a wicked, leering grin form behind my face,
just like the kind you'd see on the protagonist of a certain manga about shinigami and notebooks.

Y-KO: **— But in exchange...**

...Huh?

In exchange...?

Y-KO: I said you couldn't choose another woman
but didn't say you couldn't choose a man!
...Oh, I think they're boarding us now. Let's go,

Superhero★Sebas!

ME: **Wipe that evil smile off your face!**

That's not the kind of smile you point at your lover!
That's the smile the owner of a shinigami's notebook makes
when he announces his victory!

And that's how we came home!

* Bianca or Nera: The central choice of the game *Dragon
Quest V: Hand of the Heavenly Bride* is whether you will
marry your childhood friend Bianca or the wealthy Nera —
the ultimate dilemma. By the way, Papas (or Pankraz in the
English edition) is the main character's father, who dies
during the game.

Intellectual conversa- tion.

2007/02/25 20:35

In the school library.
Yes, the same library that has all those helpful literature, science, and history texts.

...Actually, it shames me to admit that when I was a student (okay, I still am a student),
I never got very much use out of it, so I'm not familiar with how it works...

The same library that has not a single entertaining book unrelated to study.

Yes, out of those school libraries packed full of (supposedly) intellectual textbooks...

...I have heard that some actually have copies of *My Girlfriend's a Geek*, which is centered around distinctly unintellectual conversation between Y-ko and yours truly.

...It's a thing to be grateful for.

Y-KO: ...I guess Japan's education has really broadened its horizons recently...

ME: It starts with "M," so imagine looking down the row and seeing *Macbeth* right next to *My Girlfriend's a Geek*.

Y-KO: Yeah, I don't think so.
Shouldn't it be organized by category? Then it'd go *Junai Romantica*, *My Girlfriend's a Geek*.

ME: ......*Junai Romantica*?

Y-KO: The new volume is out this month.

ME: Another BL manga?

Y-KO: Close! *Junjo Romantica* is the comic version.

ME: ...Okay, I have no idea whether that's a novel or comic,
but I do know that there's no library that stocks tons of BL!

Y-KO: Huh? If they have our book, then surely it can't be that big of a stretch, right?

ME: ......!

Y-KO: ...Right?

ME: ......

True, I guess it's not that big of a stretch...
...Wait, what?

* *Junjo/Junai* series: The *Junjo* series is a manga while the *Junai* series is a novel. The *Junjo Romantica* manga is drawn by Shungiku Nakamura, while the *Junai Romantica* novels are written by Miyako Fujisaki with illustrations and concept by Shungiku Nakamura. In fact, the *Junai* novels are a story written by the *Junjo* manga character Akihiko Usami. In other words, it's a story by Akihiko Usami told through the pen of Miyako Fujisaki. Confusing, huh?

Y-KO:	Well, if we're going to get our book put in school libraries,
	then we probably ought to have some intellectual conversation sometimes, right?
ME:	...Intellectual conversation?
Y-KO:	What's with that **Can you do that?** glance?
ME:	Ooh, close! It was actually **You can't, can you?**
Y-KO:	How rude! I'll have you know I've got an intelligent conversation or two in me!
ME:	Oh yeah?
Y-KO:	Follow me, Sebas! We're embarking on a stimulating exchange of ideas!
ME:	...No idea what you're so excited about, but I'm game.

Let's see what you've got, Y-ko.

Y-KO:	So, the yen is down!
ME:	Its exchange rate against both the dollar and the euro are brutal right now.
Y-KO:	......
ME:	......
Y-KO:	......Okay, I give up.
ME:	...Huh? What do you mean, you give up?!

Is that the end of it? Already?!
And what exactly did you think was "intellectual" about this, Y-ko?!

Y-KO: …I guess charging into battle using your specialty of economic analysis was a bad idea.

ME: This was a battle?

Y-KO: It was a mistake to challenge someone who reads the newspaper cover to cover to a discussion about the Japanese economy. If I had to make a comparison, **it was like Amuro attempting to fight the Sazabi before he had even read the manual.**

* Sazabi: A psycommu-equipped Newtype mobile suit that appears in *Mobile Suit Gundam: Char's Counterattack*. It utilizes the psychowaves emitted by Newtypes to control all the onboard systems. A very advanced craft miles beyond what was seen in the original *Mobile Suit Gundam*, where Amuro operated his first mobile suit with the manual in hand.

ME: I'm afraid your example is over my head… And isn't it normal for people to read the paper cover to cover?

Y-KO: The newspaper exists **solely for the TV guide section!**

ME: Only the TV section? No wonder you go through the paper so quickly!

I see!

The age-old mystery has finally been solved!

Plus, we get the *Nikkei* paper, which has the TV guide hidden in the middle. Must be hard to search for it!

Y-KO: Don't look at me like that, you **first-page Sebas!**

ME: First-page Sebas?!

Y-KO: First-page Sebas…Actually, wait. **That's kind of moe.**

Imagine the first page, covered with little Sebases.

ME: Actually, I think that sounds more like **horror** than **moe**…

A first page covered with Sebas.

That's an image that can only inspire fear.

If I saw it in a dream, it would be a nightmare by default.

Y-KO: Oh, crap! We've lost the topic! This isn't intellectual at all!

Did you just notice?

And I didn't realize you were still focused on your "intellectual" discussion.

Y-KO: Okay! Here we go with round two!

ME: Well, I'm game…but no giving up right off the bat like last time, okay?

Y-KO: …Did you know that Toru Furuya, who

	played the voice of Amuro Ray, also played the protagonist of *Star of the Giants*?
ME:	**I give!**

Voice actors?
And what happened to "intellectual"?

Y-KO:	And of course, you're aware that **Mr. Furuya also played the great Tuxedo Mask**, mystery thief of *Sailor Moon*?
ME:	I told you, I give up!
Y-KO:	Also, **Athrun** (*Gundam SEED*) and **Kaworu Nagisa** (*Evangelion*) **are played by the same actor.** **Murrue** (*Gundam SEED*) **was done by the person who played Misato** (*Evangelion*) **and Usagi** (*Sailor Moon*). **Also, Domon** (*Mobile Fighter G Gundam*) **and Yzak** (*Gundam SEED*) **are the same person... Oh, and I think he's also Suneo from *Doraemon*, right?**
ME:	W-well, I can at least recognize the names of some of those characters!
Y-KO:	**Plus, isn't the actor who plays Archer also the one who does Atobe?**
ME:	Are you raising the difficulty level on these references?

I've never heard of these characters before!

Y-KO: What?! You don't know them?!

ME: I can't believe you actually expected me to be familiar with them!

Y-KO: Okay, here's a hint!

ME: That's supposed to be a hint?

Y-KO: Yep. Now repeat it together with me.
Be awed at the sight of my prowess! And go!

ME: Be aw...

No way, I am not doing this.

Y-KO: **Be awed at the sight of my prowess! And go!**

ME: I told you, no way! Why do I have to repeat it?

Y-KO: Because I was surprised at how embarrassing it was to say on my own! It's not fair that I'm the only one who feels ashamed!

ME:

So you do have a sense of shame!

* *Prince of Tennis*'s Keigo Atobe and *Fate/stay night*'s Archer were both played by actor Junichi Suwabe. He's also responsible for roles in *Nana* (Kyosuke Takakura), *Nodame Cantabile* (Toru Kikuchi), *Love★Com* (Kuniumi Maitake), *Mobile Suit Gundam SEED Destiny* (Sting Oakley, Malik Yardbirds, Mars Simeon). Is there no limit to his talent?! "Be awed at the sight of my prowess" is the catchphrase of *PoT*'s Keigo Atobe.

Inhuman Monster.

2007/03/08 20:27

Well.

In the previous update, I made a statement to the effect that "school libraries would never stock anything like BL," but…

...it appears that school libraries do have BL...
I must admit that I have underestimated the diversity of our places of learning...

Y-KO: ...So school libraries do have BL...?

ME: The truth can be shocking...and did you really not know that?

Y-KO: Huh? Well, I don't go to a library to borrow books,
I just buy my own. Especially when it comes to BL.

ME: So it's been that way since you were a student?

Y-KO: When it comes to my book collection, I can probably beat your average library.
Especially when it comes to BL.

ME: That's not something I'd prefer to gloat about.

Y-KO: Want to read some?

ME: ......I'll pass, thanks.

Y-KO: What a waste. I guess I'll have to do it, then.... **Here we go.**

ME: Go ahead, be my g — **Wait a minute!**
Where did you get that book?!

Y-KO: Huh? From your bookcase.

ME: Was that always there?!

No, it definitely wasn't!
I check every week to make sure the number of books stays the same!
Especially before I have friends over to hang out!

Y-KO: Heh-heh-heh, that's my **secret skill: the mundane dust cover!**
I bet you've used that trick with your dirty materials before!

...What in the world are you doing?

ME: I've never gone to such lengths to hide a book!
Y-KO: I guess you're right... Porno mags don't have dust covers, so it wouldn't work.
ME: No, that's not the reason why I don't do it...
Y-KO: Oh, are you the DVD type? I bet if I popped open the case of *Home Alone,* I'd find a completely different disc inside!
ME: Let's try not to get too in-depth with this discussion...
...Though you're right, I do have *Home Alone* on DVD...
Y-KO: Oh, I switched the disc out.
ME: And put what inside?! When did you do this?!
Y-KO: Well, you know. Remember how you found out about me putting BL things into your pocket Six Codes case?
ME: Yes, and it was a very unpleasant surprise...

Imagine seeing the nation's code of law replaced by BL...
Thanks to that, I've been taught to check the contents of my cases habitually...

Y-KO: Plus, it goes against my *personal philosophy* to get caught twice with the same method.

I've been looking into alternate methods of hiding my BL materials.

ME: Look...The reason I don't want you to bring them into my room...

...is because I'm afraid that my friends will run across them...

Y-KO: ...Huh? Well, why do you think I'm trying to find ways to hide them?

ME: Good point! Quite salient! I never realized you were so considerate, Y-ko!

Y-KO: I know, right?

ME: **Wrong.**

I pinched her cheeks and pulled them apart.
Byoiiing.
...Of course, I made sure not to go too far.

Y-KO: **...Mwwohohhww!**

Well, I can't understand her if she talks like that.
I let go of her cheeks.

ME: ...Sorry, you were saying?

Y-KO: Stop that! What if that causes me to awaken to the pleasures of masochism?

ME: Is that what you're worried about?!

I don't think there's any cause for concern — you'll be a black-hearted sadist your entire life!

ME: I have to admit, though… I'm impressed at your hiding skills…

Y-KO: They're good, huh? I've been working on them for years.

As a matter of fact, my hiding system has **108 different techniques!**

ME: Another *Prince of Tennis* reference, I see…

As a matter of fact,
after the incredible popularity of the Atobe reference last post (so many comments!!), I had to see what the manga was like these days, and it's really gone off the deep end, hasn't it?

And to think, when I was in middle school, the most extreme move in the series was the twist serve…

Y-KO: Of course, in my own apartment, I don't bother to hide the BL at all.

ME: I feel that is a problem in and of itself.

Y-KO: Shut up. You'd be surprised at how useful this object-hiding skill is, though.
Like when I'm searching for other people's porno stuff. I already know where I'd hide it!

ME: Sounds like an incredibly pointless skill. And you didn't find any in my room, did you?

…At least, none that weren't brought in by you, yourself.

Y-KO: Exactly! I was so disappointed not to find anything!
I even abandoned my pride, crawling on the floor, looking behind the shelves,
in case there were any holes big enough for a ballpoint pen stem to fit through!

ME: Who would go to those lengths for mere porno mags?!

Y-KO: Heh... **You only say that because you have no idea of the shock of coming home one day only to learn that your family had discovered your secret stash and put it on display, neat and tidy in your bookcase... If you knew that terrible shame, you'd develop a double-stacked secret drawer to hide your goodies, too!**

ME: Wow... Is that coming from personal experience, then?

Y-KO: Oh, yes. You wouldn't believe the screaming.

ME: ... Sounds like it was pretty traumatic for you.

Y-KO: Huh? Me? No, I was the one who found the stash.

My brother was the victim.

Oh dear God!!

ME: Is that the reason why I didn't see you and your brother speaking very much when I went to visit your family last year?!

It certainly sounds like the kind of thing that could easily tear a sibling relationship into shreds!
And I have to thank God that I never had a little sister like her!

Y-KO: So, don't bother trying to hide any porno mags from here on out.
I'll find them all and hang them up in a public place while you're out of the house.

ME: # You inhuman monster!

Oh, the barbarity of it all!

Y-KO:	Oh, it's not like I told Mom and Dad about it.
ME:	...And why not?
Y-KO:	Because then I could get him to pay for my silence.
ME:	......

* Behind the drawer: A trick that Light Yagami, protagonist of *Death Note*, utilized with the desk in his bedroom.
* 108 techniques: A reference to the 108-technique Hadokyu style that appears in *Prince of Tennis*, a tennis manga that is steadily transforming into a fighting manga.

DS.

2007/03/10 14:48

The printer in my house finally gave up the ghost,
so I visited an electronic appliance store to buy a replacement.
While there, Y-ko discovered the megahit video game handheld console —
sold out everywhere for the entirety of the previous year — the Nintendo DS.

Y-KO:	Oh, hey...DS! **A Nintendo DS!!**
ME:	It sure is. First time I've ever seen one available for sale.
Y-KO:	Hang on! I'm going to buy it!

ME: Buy it...? Do you actually have the cash...?
Y-KO: No! But if I don't buy it now, I'll regret it!
             So hang on a moment!
ME: ......

...An instant decision.
If this doesn't define the term *impulse buy*, I don't know what
does...
Ignoring my exasperated looks, she finished up at the
register and returned, grinning.

Y-KO: Heh-heh-heh. Got my DS!
ME: Good for you...
             What games did you get?
Y-KO: ...I didn't get any...
             I spent all my money on the system itself...
ME: Oh...Well, it's no fun just holding the system.
             Want me to buy something?
Y-KO: Are you sure?! *Super Robo*, then! *Super
             Robo W!*
             Bonta's in it, you know! You have to get it!
             Okay?! Okay?!
ME: ...Ooh, how about this brain-training game?
             Those are popular now.
             That, or maybe this test of common
             sense...or wait, this English trainer could
             be useful.
Y-KO: Excuse me?! Are those the best choices you
             can come up with?!
             What's so fun about teasing me like that?!

ME: Well, your Alzheimer's seems to be flaring up recently.

I thought maybe you could use a bit of brain rehab.

Y-KO: Excuse me?! Since when was I senile?!

ME: Well, you've certainly forgotten our rotating schedule for doing the cooking, laundry, and garbage disposal.

Y-KO: Argh!

ME: So I'll be buying the brain trainer, then?

Y-KO: ...You're right. I have been forgetting things recently.

Oh, wait. Where did I put that thing...? I think I've just forgotten!

ME: Put what thing?

Y-KO: Well, I snuck a BL book or two into your apartment recently,

but I've completely forgotten where it went. Where could it be?

ME: Say what?! You'd better remember right now!!

Y-KO: Oh, but I think I might remember if you buy me *Super Robo W*...

ME: ....!

You are completely incorrigible!
......Oh, damn it all.

ME: ......But you only get to play one hour a day.

Y-KO: What! Why? That's so strict! It should at least be two hours!

ME:	......One and a half.
Y-KO:	Oh, fine... It's not like I'm going to hold myself to that, anyway.
	You've got a deal! Now go out there and buy me that game!
ME:	......

She just said she would ignore that rule! Out loud!
Of course, I didn't really expect her to follow my rules in the first place.
But still, I wasn't expecting her to announce it on the spot...

Without having fully accepted the situation yet, I went to the register with the trainer and *Super Robo*.

...This is terrible. If I ever have kids, I'm going to spoil them rotten.
I need to buy a book on discipline on the way home to balance this out.
Or maybe a book for new mothers.
......The fact that I think that would actually help me is kind of sad.

Y-KO:	Ooh, thanks!
	My overflowing gratitude has stimulated my brain into remembering where the BL is!
ME:	Yeah, yeah...
Y-KO:	Inside the white bag you haven't been using lately, inside the suitcase in your closet, and in the —

ME:	That's a lot! How much have you been smuggling into my home?!
Y-KO:	Don't sweat the little details.
	I plan on using them incessantly as diplomatic negotiating pieces in the future.
ME:	That's a pretty aggressive stance on diplomacy...How much were you planning on wringing out of me?
Y-KO:	Come on, don't fuss over the little stuff. It's okay.
	Plus, I know you're interested, aren't you?
ME:	Well, sure, I've always wanted to try it out a bit.
Y-KO:	Of course you have! And I'm always generous with my stuff.
	You just read all of that BL you can handle.
ME:	**What?! I was talking about the DS!**
Y-KO:	I'm glad to finally hear you admitting an honest interest.
	Of course you'd be intrigued by BL. But to hear you say you actually want to "try" it...
ME:	I have no interest! I don't want to try it!

* Bonta: The mascot character from Shoji Gatoh's series *Full Metal Panic!* Its name is based on Gonta, the character from NHK's long-running kid's program, *Dekiru Ka-Na*. Bonta appears as a hidden character in *Super Robot Taisen W* and makes a cameo in several side events within the game.

At the Bookstore.

At the bookstore.
We wandered around, pointing out books and making comments.
...But of course, the books we were speaking about weren't novels.
We were talking about manga.

ME:	Hey, it's *Ookiku Furikabutte*. Ooh, I didn't know they were making an anime of this.
Y-KO:	Hmm? Oh, **that moe manga?**
ME:	No, it's not a moe manga.
Y-KO:	**...That easily fantasizable moe manga?**
ME:	Thanks for the correction. So it still qualifies as a moe manga to you, huh?

All I see is a traditional, entertaining baseball manga.
At the very least, I'm pretty sure it's not moe.

...And it certainly doesn't cause me to have any fantasies.
I mean, I definitely don't fantasize over Momo's nice body or wish that I had a sexy coach like that in high school. No way, not me...I swear!

So stop pointing at the cover and smirking at me, Y-ko!

Y-KO:	I really like baseball manga, though. They're always entertaining.
ME:	Huh? You do? Do you know all the rules of baseball?
Y-KO:	Well, enough to enjoy the stories. Especially the part about there being nine boys for main characters.
ME:	And that's by far the most important rule to you, I'm assuming...

And that's all that Y-ko needs to enjoy something...

Y-KO:	And as long as there's an opponent to play, you're guaranteed eighteen boys, right? It's the best.
ME:	Guaranteed what...?
Y-KO:	**Guaranteed moe elements.**

That's not what they're supposed to be for!
They're supposed to be there to win the game!

Y-KO:	And you know what they say about catchers? They "play the wife" to the pitchers. Now, if that doesn't get your saliva flowing, I don't know what does.
ME:	Saliva...? Uh, I think you've got the wrong idea about this...

Y-KO: How so? There's a reason they use pitchers and catchers as a euphemism.
One of them throws, and the other "receives."

ME: That's true that they say that! It's true, but —

Y-KO: But you really have to be jealous of the girl who helps the coach manage the team.
She's got the best vantage point for all the moe goodness.

ME: Man, what a sick reason to want to be involved in a high school sport!

Y-KO: Well, it's better than if she just wanted to hook up with the guys!

ME: They're both equally distasteful!

Y-KO: The girl gets to secretly watch the coolheaded captain and the former star pitcher recovering from injury as they practice late at night. It's an **all-you-can-moe** feast.

ME: Okay, thanks to that phrase, I now think that is worse than joining so you can hook up with the players!

A female manager who joins to fantasize about the players.
...Do they exist?
......I can only pray they don't.

But then again, ever since I learned that school libraries stock BL material,
I've lost a lot of faith in the things I held for granted...

...When I get home, I'm reading *Touch* and *H2*.
Mitsuru Adachi's female managers are the best!

Y-KO: Actually, I do like baseball and all, but soccer
           manga is pretty good, too.

And she pointed at *Whistle!*
Hey, I know that one.
That really brings me back... Looks like they've made a
special reprint edition.

ME: Next is soccer, huh?
Y-KO: They have eleven players instead of nine.
ME: It all comes down to the numbers, doesn't it?
Y-KO: Well, when you have a match, then it's
           twenty-two men on the field!
           Don't you see? **All you can moe!**
ME: Would you stop using that phrase?!
           ...Wait! Is that the reason you don't like
           Prince of Tennis all that much?
           Because there are only four on the court,
           max?!
Y-KO: Huh? No, that's not why.
ME: Oh. It isn't?
Y-KO: Kikumaru can create multiple copies of
           himself, so four isn't actually the maximum.
ME: You call that a rebuttal? And please...
           multiple copies?
Y-KO: ...? What's so shocking about being able to
           multiply?

	That stuff showed up like right near the beginning of *Dragon Ball*.
ME:	You can't hold a tennis manga and a fantasy action manga to the same standards!
Y-KO:	Well, in this week's issue of *Jump,* Echizen finally mastered chi.
ME:	Chi?!
Y-KO:	Chi, or ki, is a special spiritual force that dwells within the body, which, depending on its use, can lead to an all-you-can-moe state.
ME:	Uh, I wasn't asking for a definition... And you really like that term, don't you? At least, based on the frequency of usage...
Y-KO:	Okay, I was kidding. Echizen didn't master his chi.
ME:	So you were lying...
Y-KO:	April fool!
ME:	That wasn't an April fool, and April Fools' Day has already passed.
Y-KO:	April Fools' was started in the fifteenth century, when Father April of France was sentenced to death on the first of April for telling a single lie. On the old calendar, it was April first, but in the modern age, it's actually today.
ME:	...I was wondering why that story sounded so familiar. That's the lie I told you last year on April first.
Y-KO:	It's not true?!

ME:	You mean you actually believed that?!
Y-KO:	How awful! I trusted it! And I went and told all my friends…on April first!!
ME:	**So you did know it was a lie…**

We made a tour around the store, babbling and arguing.
…When I glanced down into the basket I was carrying,
I noticed a stack of comic volumes Y-ko had slipped inside.

…This is heavy.
In fact, this is the first time I've ever used a basket in a
bookstore…

Y-KO:	Hmm…Well, that should do it.
ME:	…You know, this is really heavy. Why can't you use Amazon if you're going to buy this much?
Y-KO:	Well, some things I want to see in person before I buy. Sometimes you take a gamble based on the cover, and it turns out to be really good.
ME:	Oh…Is that how it works?
Y-KO:	A woman's heart is complex.
ME:	That saying doesn't really apply when buying a ton of manga. Plus, your reasons for buying these are anything but complex.

The answer: for moe purposes.
Three words. Not complex.

Y-KO:	Hmph. How should I describe it, then? Once again, I have bought a worthless object?
ME:	Sounds like a harsh appraisal of something you intended to enjoy.
Y-KO:	Once again, I have bought a moe object.
ME:	......

Well, that sounds about right.
We made our way to the register.

... Along the way, we passed the new releases section.

......

Y-KO:	......
ME:	......

... Y-ko and I made eye contact.
We walked faster.

Sped through the new releases section.

... Whew.
Once we had made it past, we breathed a sigh of relief.

Y-KO:	......I'll never get used to it.
ME:	......Nope. Sure won't.

For some reason, I can't help but speed up my pace whenever I pass by *My Girlfriend's a Geek* in the bookstore...

I wonder if other blog writers who have been published in book form feel the same way...

Sumomomo, Momomo.

2007/05/13 23:23

The other day at Y-ko's house.

— Looks like dinner's ready.
Better let Y-ko know.
When I headed into her room, she was facing her computer, back to the door.

She was in the same spot when I came over, too.
Must be busy with work...

Is she...humming?
Wait, now she's singing...

Y-KO: **Let's make a baby ♪.**
ME: ....
Y-KO: Tra-la-la-la, lun-lun-lun.
ME: ....
Y-KO: Tra-la-la-la-la-la, loo-loo-loo-loo.

...What did she just say?
What did she sing in that rhythmical manner?

Still unsure whether or not I should comment on what I had
just heard,
I reached out and tapped Y-ko's shoulder from behind.

ME: Umm...Dinner's ready...
Y-KO: La-la — huh? Oh, thanks.

She pulled the buds out of her ears and turned to me.
...Should I say something now?
......I guess I probably should.

ME: What were you just singing?
Y-KO: Huh? What? I was singing?

She wasn't even aware of it?
Well, thank goodness this didn't happen in the workplace.

ME: **...You seemed to be very upbeat about making babies, unless I misheard you...**

Y-KO: Oh, that was an anime theme song. I was just watching it.
It's the *Sumomomo, Momomo* song. It goes, "Let's make a baby ♪.
The song is really catchy. You'll find yourself humming it unconsciously.

ME: Sumo...momomo...?

I don't really get it.
The only thing I can say is that the lyrics are pretty outrageous.
Is it based on an eroge?

...And hey, I thought you were working

Y-KO: It's pretty neat. Unfortunately, YouTube's video quality isn't that great, so it's a good thing that Nico Nico Video's is much better.

ME: Okay...So you were watching anime on a video site.

Y-KO: Yeah. I'll regret it if I miss a series and it turns out to be a classic, no?
That's why it's so handy to have YouTube and Nico Nico Video.

	And let me tell you, this *Sumomomo, Momomo* series is a hidden gem.
ME:	A hidden gem, huh?
Y-KO:	I only meant to take a little peek, and I ended up blowing through all twenty-two episodes.
ME:	Through twenty-two episodes?! At a half hour each episode, that's...eleven hours?! Have you been up all night?!
Y-KO:	Huh? Yeah, but I took a caffeine drink, so I'm good. My eyes are wide open, see? So pumped.
ME:	You used an all-night caffeinated drink so you could watch anime?! Even though it takes you coffee just to make it through overtime at work?! Yikes, your eyes are bloodshot!
Y-KO:	Huh? Oh, they are? Well, I cried a lot after the final episode...
ME:	......

So it has a ridiculous opening song, and it makes you cry? Never doubt the power of Japanimation, I guess!

Y-KO:	And I love opening themes that are insidiously catchy. **Let's make a baby** ♪.
ME:	Okay, first of all? Don't sing that song when we're eating. I mean, with those lyrics and all... ...So let's dig in before it gets cold...

— Several days later.

Y-KO: Check it out! I bought *Sumomomo, Momomo*!
        I got all the DVDs and the manga volumes
        that are out.

ME: I didn't realize you liked *Sumomomo,
        Momomomo* that much!!

Y-KO: One too many *mo*'s.

ME: And the amount you spend on anime has one
        too many zeroes!

Y-KO: Touché... whatever. I love mail order, though.
        It would be pretty hard to walk out of a store
        with all those DVDs and books.

ME: ...Why? Because it's embarrassing?

Y-KO: No, it's heavy. Think of how bulky that would
        be to carry home.

ME: Oh, so that's the issue...

Y-KO: What? You'd prefer if I bought them in person?
        You'd be the one carrying it on the way
        home... Trust me, it's heavy.

ME: What? You mean you were actually being
        considerate to me?!

Y-KO: Of course. That's why I ordered them.
        Plus, don't you know that young boys in
        puberty just love this kind of manga?

ME: ......I'm not sure how I feel about the fact
        that the manga boys in puberty love happens
        to be the kind of manga you love... Plus, if
        you've seen the whole series, why do you
        need the DVDs?

Y-KO: Well, for one thing, the quality is really bad on those video sites.
And the DVD quality is amazing in comparison. Not that I've watched these ones yet.

ME: So you're happy just by purchasing them...

Y-KO: It's always well and good when you decide to just splurge on a DVD, but you end up watching it only two or three times...
Anyway, you wanna read it? It's good!

ME: Right...

Y-KO: Look, there's a pretty girl who pushes her way into the guy's house and acts as his wife and does everything for him!
Isn't that like every guy's ultimate dream?
Oh, and, Sebas, I want some hot cocoa.

ME: ......A girl who does everything for the guy...What a dream...

— Why am I always the one doing all the work...?

Of course, I'm still happy with where I am.

Dream.
2007/05/14 15:35

Once again, at Y-ko's house.
As I lazily gazed at the titles of manga packed into her bookshelf,
I noticed a familiar title: *Saikano*.
I read it in high school because I heard it was incredibly sad...
But all I really remember was that it was surprisingly sexy.

...Well, er.
I was at that kind of age.
Being unfamiliar with manga of that category, I found this experience very shocking.

Y-KO:	Hmm? What's up?
ME:	I've read this manga. This one here. That takes me back.

Y-KO:	Really? You've got good taste, sir. How was it? Did you cry?
ME:	...Well, it was definitely moving.
Y-KO:	Hmph. You didn't cry?
ME:	Unfortunately, it didn't move me to tears.
Y-KO:	...You coldhearted brute.
ME:	So I'm coldhearted because I didn't cry over a comic book?
Y-KO:	If you don't cry over this manga, there is something wrong with you as a person! I've read it dozens of times, and I still bawl my eyes out!
ME:	I'm just saying, I don't know if that makes much sense...
Y-KO:	In fact, just reading the first chapter now reminds of the finale, and I cry!!
ME:	Okay, now I'm positive there's something wrong with you...
Y-KO:	I've made up my mind! I'm going to give you a crash course in human emotions! Soon you'll be as passionate, heartfelt, and hot-blooded as anyone!
ME:	Hot-blooded...?

She makes it sound like my attack power is about to be doubled.

ME:	Anyway, how do you decide if a person is passionate or frigid based on their reaction to a manga?

Y-KO:	Well, how else are you going to judge?
ME:	Actually, I think there are plenty of better ways to determine that...
Y-KO:	Like whether or not you give your school lunch to an abandoned puppy on a rainy day?
ME:	Uh, wow...That is the corniest, most cliché idea I've ever heard...
Y-KO:	The problem is, sadly enough, I've never run across one of those mangalike situations in real life.
ME:	Can't say I have, either.

Plus, I thought they forbade taking home school food as a measure against food poisoning.

Y-KO:	Also, in my experience, I've never run into a pretty girl carrying toast at a blind corner and later found out that she was a transfer student about to start at my school. ...In fact, I've never ever seen anyone running with toast in their mouth.
ME:	Oh, I've run with toast in my mouth before.
Y-KO:	Really? While shouting, "I'll be late, I'll be late"?
ME:	No, it was in a bread-eating race at a school competition.
Y-KO:	That's completely different...
ME:	You know, there are lots of things that happen often in manga but never in real life.

Y-KO: True…I've never been summoned to an
          alternate dimension to be a hero.
          I've never snuck into a military lab and
          ridden on a secret weapon vehicle to
          escape.
          Even though it was my childhood dream…
          If it doesn't happen soon, then I'm afraid that
          when it does happen,
          I'll be too late to be the main character age-
          wise.
          I'd have to be the sexy support member.

Heroes and top secret vehicles.
Honestly, if those are the most realistic examples you can
come up with…
Doesn't she have any fantasies that are even remotely
plausible?

ME: To be picky, your weight might even exclude
          you from sexy support staff.
Y-KO: ……Heh-heh-heh.
ME: **Ouch, ouch, ouch! Not my ear;
          that hurts! I'm sorry!**

She had dug her nails into my ear.
…It's kind of a weird sensation…
Oh no. What if I get a taste for it?

Y-KO: But why does the pilot end up being an
          ordinary, innocent civilian?

And of course, the rival ends up being the main character's childhood friend.

ME: I'm sure they just used that to make the story exciting.

Y-KO: By coincidence, the civilian protagonist's colony is attacked.

By coincidence, the attacker is his friend; by coincidence, he gets in a combat vehicle; and by coincidence, he happens to have a special power —

ME: *Gundam SEED*, right?

Y-KO: — It's an amazing setup.

The love that blossomed between the two enemies, Kira and Athrun, was so passionate.

ME: Kira and Athrun...?

I thought the romances were between Kira and Lacus and Athrun and Cagalli.

...Isn't that right, Y-ko?

ME: You seem to have accepted the coincidences fairly readily...

Y-KO: Well, it was coincidence that brought us together, too.

It's a wonderful thing!

ME: ......

I wish she would have used the word *fate*...
Oh well, not that it matters.

Y-KO: Man, I wish I could ride a Gundam, even if it has to be by coincidence.

ME: Your fantasies seem to have a very masculine edge to them.

                     Heroes, Gundam pilots, and so on. Don't you have any feminine desires?

I doubt she imagines herself working in a bakery or a patisserie.

... But if she does have them ... what would they be?

Y-KO: Hmm? What, you want girlish ideas?

                     Of course, I'm like any girl. I've imagined that I was a princess in a past life.

ME: A princess, huh? Well, it's definitely more girly than Gundam.

Y-KO: And in that past life, the hero came into my life.

ME: And you lived happily ever after?

Y-KO: No. **That hero in the past life** (male) **and the evil sorcerer** (male) **experienced a burning, forbidden love ... which I spied upon from the shadows.**

ME: Wow, that's some epic BL! But if that was the case, where's the necessity for you to be a princess in your past life?

Y-KO: **Silence, Sebas.** There's no point to having a past life if I'm not the main character.

But then again, speaking of heroes...

ME: ...? What is it?

Y-KO: I get the feeling that in your past life, you were more of a Sebas than a hero.

In fact, I'm positive that you served my noble household.

ME: **...So I've been stuck in the same position since my previous life...?**

Should I be pleased that I at least haven't been paired with the evil sorcerer (male)?

...But I digress. I see now that it's been my fate to serve this person since my prior life.

Past life, present life, and I'd put good money down that in my future life I will be Sebas as well.

......Huh? Strange, I feel happy about that?

Y-KO: But enough about me. What about you? Don't you think about that stuff? **Outside of being a superhero.**

ME: Would you please just drop that topic, already? Please...

But of course, I have thought about that stuff before.

Y-KO: I see. Please, elaborate.

ME: ...For example...Let's see, like going out with an older lady and being cooked some delicious food.

Y-KO: ......Ack.

ME: Maybe going out with a mature lady and doing this...and that?
...Of course, that wasn't all that long ago. In fact, I think of it often these days...

Y-KO: ......Wh-what?

ME: ......

Y-KO: ......

ME: ......

Y-KO: ......

—I was so young in those days...

Y-KO: What? Excuse me...What's the deal?! Are you saying this is my fault?!

Trouble Descends.

2007/05/16 21:20

I finished buying the groceries for dinner and returned to Y-ko's place.
After opening the door with the spare key, I was met with the sight of Y-ko
frozen in the Kamehameha position.

— Awkward.
This really feels awkward.

ME:	......
Y-KO:	......
ME:	...What are you doing?
Y-KO:	Ha...ha-ha-ha. You caught me in an embarrassing situation.

And laughing shyly, she pulled the earphones out.
...Watching anime on her computer again, I see.

ME:	...*Dragon Ball* this time?
Y-KO:	Grr, how can you tell?!
ME:	Well, it was pretty obvious from the pose.
Y-KO:	...I was watching the scene where Gohan shows Videl how to float, and I thought I might be able to do it, too.
ME:	Well, I can understand the intention...
Y-KO:	So I was just making a "wouldn't it be nice to fly" kind of pose...see?
ME:	See? See what...?
	Plus, that was clearly the Kamehameha pose.
	I think you'd be dismayed at the results of pulling off one of those in your room.
Y-KO:	Oh, come on. Of course I can't shoot a Kamehameha. Are you that dumb?
ME:	......
Y-KO:	......?

She called me dumb.
Someone who was just making the Kamehameha pose in her room called me dumb.

... If I had Saiyan blood running in my veins,
I would have gone Super Saiyan after that comment.

Y-KO: Videl is really quite the tsundere, by the way.
ME: Oh.
Y-KO: To think, a character that fits my aesthetic
           vision perfectly, made over a decade ago!
           Never underestimate the power of Akira
           Toriyama. I've made up my mind!
           From now on, I want to be just like Videl.
ME: ...As long as it doesn't cause me grief, I'm
           all for it.
Y-KO: Of course it won't cause you grief. It'll be
           fine.
           But all of that aside, Sebas...
ME: Yes?
Y-KO: I want you to strike the Great Saiyaman pose.
ME: What kind of harassment is this?!

Look at that, a whole wheelbarrow full of grief!

Y-KO: Uh, you can do his f...foo...hyoo...hyoojon
           form.
ME: Wrong! It's pronounced "fusion," not
           "hyoojon."
Y-KO: That's what I said, fusion. Do it.

ME:	No. Plus, I don't want to bother the people downstairs.
Y-KO:	Okay, fine. Do it in midair.
ME:	I can't! Only anime people can fly! And what the hell is with this obsession today?!
Y-KO:	I got an e-mail from your mother today.
ME:	.........And?
Y-KO:	**I hear that at the elementary school talent festival, you and a friend struck the fusion pose.**
ME:	Ah...ah...

Mom......
You are ruining my life......
How could you tell her about that?
It's so embarrassing, I'd managed to forget the whole thing, but you just had to go and tell her, of all people...

Y-KO:	Fusion in front of the entire student body. What a gutsy move.
ME:	Well, what else should I have done? *Dragon Ball* was all the rage back then... We put lots of *Shōnen Jump* jokes into our script for laughs... And I was also the only person who was the right height compared to the other person.
Y-KO:	Wow, you even had the heights figured out... I bet I could get along great with the person who wrote your script.

...Oh, but that's not all I heard about.

Apparently, when you were in kindergarten, you practiced in front of the mirror, trying to move faster than your reflection.

ME: ......

...Mom...

Have I done something to make you hate me?

Y-KO: And when dinner came around, you told your dad,

"I moved faster than the mirror! Will I be a superhero now?"

ME: ......

Y-KO: Oh, would you stop slumping on all fours on the floor?
             That's not the pose I was asking for. Great Saiyaman or fusion pose only, please.

Sigh...

I haven't seen Y-ko having this much fun in ages!

Dammit!

Why do I feel such despair?!

Y-KO: Man...This is all much too cute.
             Why didn't you tell me about your adorable past?

ME: Why would anyone willingly drudge up their embarrassing past?

Y-KO: Oh, you rascal. Big sister's very proud of you. You were such a little sweetheart!

ME: ......!

Y-KO: But now it's time to return to your mischievous past!
I'll be Great Saiyaman number two, so you handle number one's pose."

ME: Absolutely not!! You have zero intention of making that pose, do you?!

Y-KO: Damn, busted.

ME: I knew it...

Y-KO: Don't let it bother you...Ooh, got another message. What does this one say...?
Ohh, it sounds like she still has video of that talent show presentation.

ME: What?! Why does she still have that?!
And more importantly, what kind of e-mails have you been trading with my mom?!

Y-KO: **What kind? The Top 100 Most Embarrassing Stories involving you.**

ME: Mom...What are you doing to me...?

Of all the horrible shocks!
My own mother has turned to the enemy's side!!

Y-KO: **– Oh, and I've been thanking**

her for these stories by reporting more embarrassing tales about you (in the present) in return.

ME: ......

Th...this is no time to be crying!!
Hang in there, me...Hang in there!!

"Happi-ness."

2007/07/30 21:00

As I returned home from my work training session,
I found an almost shockingly excited Y-ko.
Full beam on her lips, comic magazine in her hand.

Comic B's Log.

— The comic magazine that, beginning this month, will run Rize Shinba's manga version of *My Girlfriend's a Geek*.

Y-KO: You're finally home! It's about time, Sebas! The magazine that has the manga in it has arrived!! Here, look!!

And she shoved the magazine under my nose.
...Oh, wow. Right on the cover. *My Girlfriend's a Geek*.

ME: ......Uhh, for starters, I'm home.

Y-KO: Welcome back! So, **would you like manga?! Would you like manga?! Would you like manga?! Or would you prefer manga?!**

ME: You seem really excited, Y-ko...

Y-KO: Are you kidding?! I've been turned into a manga!
How can I stay calm? **How shan't I stay calm?!**

ME: ...That doesn't make any sense.

Y-KO: I'm serious! What should we do, Sebas? This is amazing!
I've finally fulfilled my longtime dream and become two-dimensional!
And I look so pretty! What's going on? Is this a dream? If it's a dream...

And she brandished the magazine at me.
What's she going to do? Hit me with it? With the corner?!

ME: Careful! Not the corner! Those thick
           magazines hurt when you hit with the corner!!
Y-KO: ...Oh, I'm only kidding. I wouldn't hit you
           with such a valuable magazine.
           What if I snapped something?
ME: Like...my bones?
Y-KO: No, like the spine of the magazine.
ME: Ouch, that hurts my heart! I think you may
           have snapped my heart in two!!
Y-KO: Oh good. If it hurts, that proves that this isn't
           a dream.

......

Okay. Hang in there, me.

ME: ...Putting that aside, how was it?
           What do you think of the manga edition?
Y-KO: The collection of family treasures that is
           passed down through generations has just
           grown to accept a new article.

....

Family treasure already? Of course, that's pretty much how I
felt about it, too.

ME: Well, it's certainly an amazing thing to be the
           main character of a manga.
           ...But the idea of a multigeneration family
           treasure is just as wild.
           My family doesn't have any of those.

Y-KO: Oh, there's all sorts of stuff. **I've also got all the necklaces and shoes you gave me, and the stub of the first movie we saw together, and the notes with messages that you left for me.**

ME: ......

Y-KO: What's up? Your face is red.

ME: ...Would you not surprise me with a **dere** ambush like that?

Y-KO: Sorry, can't help ya. Making you blush is an intense pleasure of mine.
Heh-heh-heh, and your face is red as a beet, Sebas!

You're right — it is!
But so is yours, Y-ko!
I guess you've forgotten that saying those corny lines makes you blush, too!

...Damn, she is too cute!

So once I had finished reading the manga edition of *My Girlfriend's a Geek*, already added to Y-ko's list of family treasures (?), she called out to me from behind.

Y-KO: Let me see that, if you're done. I want to read it again.

ME: Hang on a minute. I want to read it again, too.

You've probably read it dozens of times this afternoon, haven't you?

Y-KO: Wow, look at that! Sebas, completely engrossed in a shōjo manga! Finally... **Finally my teachings have born fruit!!**

ME: Say whatever you like. I'm not giving it back.

Y-KO: Boo! Give it here! That's my family treasure!

ME: Your family treasure is my family treasure, dear. You'll just have to wait a little longer.

...The manga edition is seriously incredible, though. I can definitely see why Y-ko was so pumped up!

Y-KO: ......

— Okay, done rereading.
I turned back to her and gave her the magazine.

Y-KO: ...Sebas.

ME: What?

Y-KO: Say something funny, Sebas.

ME: What kind of a request is that?! Something funny?!

Y-KO: ...Hmm. Yeah, that sounds like what my Sebas would respond with, too.

ME: ...My Sebas? Too?

Y-KO: Well, there was a scene in *Lucky Star* where Konata said,
"Say something funny, Sebastian."

ME: Huh?...So what did the Sebas say?

Y-KO: He said, "No way, I can't!"

ME: Of course he did...So, Y-ko, why don't you say something funny?

Y-KO: **The other day, I packed my boyfriend's Photobucket account full of BL images, but he hasn't noticed yet because he never checks it. I'm a little bit worried, because I know he takes his laptop to his work training every single day.**

ME: That is definitely not a funny story! But I want to hear any other stories you have like that! Spit them out! All of them! Or else something terrible will happen!!

Y-KO: Something terrible? What? Is someone going to get hurt?

ME: Yes, me!

Y-KO: Okay, that one was kind of funny. Whenever you make a really goofy pose, it usually elicits a chuckle.

ME: That wasn't for humor! I am dead serious!

Y-KO: Now, take that laptop packed full of my love, and go survive another day of your harrowing on-the-job training!

ME: I don't want that kind of sinister, evil love! Oh my God! It really is packed full of BL images!!

Y-KO: Love has to drive a hard bargain, Sebas.

ME: I don't need this kind of love!

Y-KO: You're saying you can't accept my love?!

	Even though you all but proposed to me right here and now?!
ME:	**Proposed...?** Oh, you mean when I said that your family treasures were my family treasures?
Y-KO:	...Oh, so you were aware of it?
ME:	No, I just saw your face get red, and I thought, "Crap!"
Y-KO:	Why didn't you say anything after that, then?!
ME:	I dunno. I got curious as to what happens next in "Sepatte Takuro."
Y-KO:	**Who are you, me?!** Yuiko Ameya?! Dammit, Sebas! Make me some tea! It is now my reading time!
ME:	Certainly, madam.

I picked out two matching cups and poured the boiling water.

I pulled her favorite tea bag out of the cupboard and inserted it into the cup.

I put the lid over the cup to let it steam and waited two minutes.

Y-KO:	....
ME:	...What is it?
Y-KO:	I was just thinking, you're getting the hang of the tea preparation thing.
ME:	Well, it's still just tea bags. Of course, I could practice a more traditional method if it would make you happy.

Y-KO: Mm, nah. This way is good enough…

             Plus, I've been thinking about it, and it seems
             like all of my dreams have been coming true
             since I met you.
ME: Pardon?
Y-KO: Did you know that I've always wanted a
             Sebas-style boyfriend who would make me
             tea?
             And just today, my dream of entering the
             world of manga came true.

As she said this, Y-ko pointed at the cover of the magazine in
her hand.
On the cover, smiling up at me,
was the manga version of Y-ko — Yuiko Ameya.

Y-KO: And look how beautiful I am…What do I do
             now?
             Most of my dreams in life have all come true.
ME: Really? Well, I'm happy for you.
             ……If I've made it this far, I might as well
             make all your life dreams come true.
Y-KO: ……
ME: ……
Y-KO: …Would you stop making my heart beat with
             surprises like that?
ME: Sorry, no can do.

…I just love seeing her blush.

Y-KO: ...Okay, then. I guess you *will* have to make them come true.

ME: Leave it to me. I can promise I'll give all the effort I have.

Y-KO: Really?

ME: Really.

I looked into her eyes and nodded firmly.

Y-KO: And what if I told you to make me happy?

ME: I will do it.

...Wait, what? Why did I give an instant response?
She said she wanted me to make her happy, not that she wanted to be happy, right?
Was that question...what I thought it was?

Ummm...

Y-KO: ...By the way.

ME: ...**By the way?**

ME: When you say, make you happy…

Y-KO: To be more precise,

I've been having trouble making room for all my BL books, so I'd like you to keep some of them in your apartment,

that's all!

ME: ……

Y-KO: And if you went on a BL shopping spree and decided to fill the place with your own material, that would make me even happier!

ME: And it would make me miserable!

Y-KO: Oh, please. You know you're happy just having me in your life.

ME: How did you know that?!

Y-KO: …How did I know? Uh, because…

ME: ……

Y-KO: Your face is red, Sebas.

ME: So is yours, Y-ko.

Happy Ending.

2007/++/++ 00:00

The stroke of midnight — the date changes.
Today is my girlfriend's long-awaited birthday.
The present is paid for and prepared; the only question is when to hand it over.
I started by congratulating her on her lucky day.

ME: Happy birthday, my dear.

Y-KO: Mm, thanks. Alas, now the gap between us grows one year wider.

ME: Oh, only for a few months. You'll be back to a two-year lead in a few months.

Y-KO: That's all right for now, but what happens when I'm about to turn thirty and you're still in your youthful twenties? Of course, I don't *really* mind.
             I like the sound of "younger boyfriend." And you like older ladies, don't you?

ME: It's true that I have no qualms with the older women…

But it's not like that's my bag, y'know?
I would have fallen in love with Y-ko even if she was younger than me.

— Of course, I don't say this stuff out loud.

But enough about that.

ME:	It's funny, you don't really have that older woman image, though.
Y-KO:	What?! Why not?! What about me doesn't fit the archetype?!
ME:	Maybe when we first met, but not anymore… I'm just saying, you don't really give off that "big sister" aura…
Y-KO:	…Hmph. What does that make me, then?
ME:	Umm…More like a **master,** if anything.
Y-KO:	Hmmmm. Master, huh…? I like the ring of it! Sebas! From now on, you will call me master!
ME:	What?! Is that really what you want?! I was hoping your reaction would be more like, **"Oh no, is that how you've seen me all this time? I'll do the cooking and laundry from now on!"**
Y-KO:	Nope, sorry. Besides, I like your cooking.
ME:	……Thank you. I like your cooking, too, though.
Y-KO:	Oh, all right, then. I'll make tomorrow's dinner.
ME:	Nope, sorry. The date has changed, and it's now your birthday. That means I'm cooking tonight.

Y-KO:	......
ME:	...What's up?
Y-KO:	...A thought just occurred to me. You don't want to let me cook, do you?
ME:	......

...Busted.

Laundry is one thing, but when it comes to food, sometimes I just like to give her a bit of a hard time.

At some point in time, I realized that having someone whole-heartedly enjoy my cooking was a greater pleasure than I ever could have imagined.

Y-KO:	...What are you now, a housewife?
ME:	All thanks to your long and tireless training.
Y-KO:	Heh...Nice one, me. But wait a second. Does that mean I no longer have the option of being that babelike older lady who's also a killer cook?
ME:	I guess that would be the case.
Y-KO:	Damn...Oh well! I guess I can try to seduce you through other avenues of attack, then!
ME:	Oh? Like what?
Y-KO:	**Big Brother Sebas! I can't figure out my homework. Will you help me do it?**
ME:	The little sister method...?

Plus, Sebas is bad enough, but **Big Brother Sebas** is just ludicrous.

There has to be a less surreal nickname to use.

And in the end, it's always me doing everything!

Y-KO: It's a question where I have to debate whether Kira is seme or uke for at least four hundred words...

ME: I've never even heard of such an assignment!

And even if it was real, I would never want a little sister who asked her big brother for help on it!

Y-KO: Huh? It's the same question I asked my older brother.

......

Of course.

She would do this.

She's a little sister with a Gundam otaku for a brother.

ME: ...And I'm sure you traumatized your brother for life.

Y-KO: Actually, this is what he said:

"Save those questions for that boyfriend of yours..."

ME: Why?! Damn, I didn't know your brother was my enemy, too!

> I believed in my heart of hearts that he of all people would sympathize with me!

Y-KO: But it was just a one-sided crush all along.

ME: That's a very misleading way to phrase that emotion.

Y-KO: Oh...was it requited?

ME: There was no love to begin with!!
And can you imagine a more disturbing love triangle?!

Your boyfriend and your older brother in love with each other.

...Why the hell am I thinking about this?

Y-KO: ...Kinda hot, actually.

ME: Kinda not hot, actually! Kinda really gross!

Y-KO: But there's still one problem.

ME: Oh, trust me, there's well more than one problem with that...

Y-KO: **Both you and my brother seem like the uke type.**

ME: ......

If there's a real problem, it's Y-ko's fundamental fujoshi nature...
Why are we even talking about this?
I'm in my girlfriend's room on her birthday, and we're talking about possibly the most inappropriate topic imaginable for such an occasion.

Of course, it's not like I haven't grown completely used to this by now.
I'm used to it,
I enjoy it, and I'm happy with it.
No matter what the topic is, when I'm with my girlfriend, I'm happy.
The days that pass by are all incredibly precious to me.

Y-KO:	— Hmm, but you know...
ME:	?
Y-KO:	I'm amazed that you still love me.
ME:	... What?
Y-KO:	I mean, look at me. I'm not as good at cooking as I pretend...
	In fact, I just let you do all of the cooking.
	My boobs are small, I don't really act my age, and I'm selfish.
	Most of all —
ME:	— You're a fujoshi?
Y-KO:	......Yeah. I'm a fujoshi.
	It's weird for me to say this myself...but sometimes I get worried.
	Like is it right for things to be this way?
ME:	......
Y-KO:	I feel bad, but I'll probably keep being a fujoshi, keep being selfish, and keep calling you Sebas forever.
ME:	Great.
Y-KO:	But because of that, I think I'll also love you forever.

...I guess that makes it an equivalent exchange?

ME: I see.

Equivalent exchange.

It's a phrase I've heard from Y-ko's lips countless times since I began dating her,
but I never imagined it would be used in such a serious context...

Y-KO: I guess all I'm saying is, "Here's looking at more time with you, Sebas."

ME: Y-ko.

Y-KO: Oh, come on. It was hard for me to say all that, so don't give me your usual snappy comebacks.

ME: Actually, I wasn't going to snap at you... I was just going to say that, although it's not exactly as if I'm doing this to return the favor for those nice things you just said... I have something I want to tell you, too.

And I pulled out the present I had hidden for this moment.
I put the little case into Y-ko's hand.
— The case that held a ring fitted to her finger size.

ME: I want you to be with me forever.

Y-KO: ......

ME: ......

Y-KO: ...Okay, I think pulling this stunt at a time like this is uncalled for.

ME: You think so?

Y-KO: I mean, this case... It's what I think it is, right?

ME: Yes. Exactly what it looks like.

Y-KO: ...Just one question.

ME: What is it?

Y-KO: Which finger should I put the ring on?

And with a devilish little grin, she opened the case up in front of me.

— Oh, come on.
The answer should be obvious.

I silently pulled the ring out of the case and took her left hand.

ME: This one.

And I slipped it on her left ring finger.

Y-KO: — Thank you.

ME: No problem.

Y-KO: ...Didn't you ever learn that you shouldn't make a girl cry?

ME: I did.

Y-KO: Well, you failed…stupid Sebas. I ought to scold you.

ME: I'm sorry.

Y-KO: ……But just this time, I'll forgive you. Tears of joy don't count.

ME: Oh good. You're scary when you're mad.

Y-KO: Argh! Come here and let me use your shirt.
I'll mess it up with tears and snot.

ME: Of course, madam. Here you are.

And I pulled her close to me.

— Since the day I met her…
I've been exasperated by the amount of manga she buys.
I've been shocked at the BL she smuggles into my apartment.
I've been impressed by her expansive knowledge of anime.
I've been aroused by the maid uniform she wears.

I'm sure that in the future, I'll continue to be manipulated by her fujoshi hobbies.
And I'm sure that slowly but surely, her tastes will rub off on me.
Day by eccentric, precious day.

I'm sure I'll always be by her side as her Sebas.
After all, even in my arms, she said —

"Here's looking at a long life ahead, Sebas."

— And her head finally raised again, I answered,

"As you say, Y-ko."

Afterword.

So.
My Girlfriend's a Geek reaches its happy ending.

So many things have happened since I met her,
and I've learned so many things as well.
Fujoshi, BL, manga, anime, video games, cosplay —
At first it was a never-ending string of shocks...

But as I spent more and more time with her,
all of those things became ordinary and familiar,
until everyday life with my girlfriend became something
precious and essential to me.

We had our fights.
I made her cry on occasion.
We even had a long-distance relationship when she
transferred.
(When she nonchalantly said, "I've been ordered to switch
locations," I had no idea what to do...)

But after that, after I had grown used to her impish grin and
manipulative ways, the thought of life without her became
unbearable.

I made full use of the degree that I worked hard to obtain
and nearly forced myself into a job in her new city.

She cried again.

And because of all that, both of us are still smiling.
I have no doubt that in the future,
I will continue to be manipulated.

But to me, that has become the very definition of happiness.

She has brought so much happiness into my life.
This time, it's my turn to return the favor.

The ring sparkles on her finger.
I can only hope that this will make her happy...

— But I suppose that will all depend on me, going forward.

To everyone who has supported *My Girlfriend's a Geek*,
from the bottom of my heart, thank you.

This is the happy ending for the blog,
but our lives will continue beyond this point.

Y-ko and I will do our very best to lead happy lives together,
so I hope you will continue to cheer for us.

August 1, 2007

My Girlfriend's a Geek.
Pentabu, Y-ko

Notes/ Glossary

Adachi, Mitsuru A veteran manga artist who specializes in stories about youth sports. His baseball epics *Cross Game*, *H2*, and most particularly the early 1980s *Touch* are famous for their deft touch and introspective nature, in contrast to the flashy and exaggerated style of most sports manga.

Amuro Amuro Ray, the hero of the original *Mobile Suit Gundam*.

Angel's Egg A novel (and its subsequent film adaptation) by Yuka Murayama. Not to be confused with the surrealistic animated film of the same name by Mamoru Oshii.

BL "Boy's Love." A recent term synonymous with *yaoi* whose usage has largely replaced the other within Japan. Unlike *yaoi*, which could refer strictly to self-published manga parodies (*dōjinshi*) placing heterosexual characters from established stories in homosexual relationships, BL is considered more of a catchall term encompassing original and commercial works as well.

Commodore Perry U.S. Naval Commodore Matthew Perry was responsible for convincing the Japanese to open their borders to the West in the 1850s, an agreement which is listed among the unequal treaties, a series of one-sided treaties which the colonial powers of the West used to exploit the weaker countries of the East. (Yes, despite the author's puzzlement, Perry was a central figure in the unequal treaties.)

Cyborg 009 A classic manga/anime series by Shotaro Ishinomori about an evil organization that turns ordinary people into powerful cyborgs. The nine cyborgs escape their wicked masters and band together to save humanity.

Death Note   A megahit manga series that was published in *Weekly Shōnen Jump*. The story of an otherwordly notebook that would kill the person whose name was written on its pages, it also spawned an anime series and live-action film.

dōjinshi   Self-published manga (or sometimes prose) that are widely bought and sold at conventions such as Comiket. Most dōjinshi are sexual in nature, and most are parodies based on existing series, though exceptions to both of these categories exist.

Doraemon   An iconic children's manga by Fujiko F. Fujio starring lazy and flawed fourth grader Nobita and his friend, the blue cat robot Doraemon. Through Doraemon's magic pocket full of tools, Nobita and his school friends embark on various adventures, usually with some moral lesson at the end. Because the story is so iconic, people are often associated with the characters' different archetypes; that is, to describe someone as a Nobita is to suggest that he is a weak loser or dweeb, while someone who is selfish and bullying might be compared to the character Gian.

Dragon Ball   Akira Toriyama's classic series, which is virtually synonymous with anime and manga throughout the world. Does this really need to be explained?

Dragon Quest   The most popular and long-running role-playing game series in Japan. The release of a new title in the series causes such a rush of activity and absences from work or school nationwide that the government has pressured the game's makers to release them during holidays.

eroge   A Japanese abbreviation for "erotic game," referring to computer games with erotic content. These usually take the form of adventure games with still illustrations for graphics and simple text dialogue, but some can have quite elaborate and literary stories. Some of the most popular eroge have been adapted for consoles like the PlayStation and even made into anime series (usually with the explicit sexual content removed).

fujoshi   A self-deprecating term referring to female fans of yaoi (or BL). The word is a homophone of the Japanese word for "respectable lady," but the character for "woman" is replaced with the character for "rotten," thus forming a word that means "rotten girl." This refers to the supposedly "rotten" thoughts and fantasies that fujoshi have about characters or people in gay relationships, which would not normally occur. In recent years, the term's definition has been loosened slightly to sometimes include female otaku without a strong predilection for BL. For example, some real-life self-identified fujoshi may claim that despite her fujoshi labeling, Y-ko shares more characteristics with regular female otaku than fujoshi.

Hagaren   The abbreviation of *Haga*ne no *Ren*kinjutsushi, the Japanese title of *Fullmetal Alchemist*.

Haruhi Suzumiya   A series of comedic light novels by Nagaru Tanigawa in which the titular main character forms a brigade with her school classmates to investigate mysterious events. Later adapted into manga and anime form. Available now from Yen Press!

Honda, Takayoshi   An award-winning Japanese novelist. His short story "Yesterdays" was adapted into a film.

Honey and Clover   A comedy/drama/romance manga and anime series by Chika Umino detailing the lives of a group of art students living in the same apartment building. The character of Takemoto is a mellow "nice guy" who is unable to act on his emotions. In contrast, Morita is an unpredictable eccentric who acts in mysterious ways.

Laputa: Castle in the Sky   A 1986 anime film (released as *Castle in the Sky* in English) directed by Hayao Miyazaki. As the first full-length feature from the incredibly prestigious Studio Ghibli, this film is perhaps more beloved than any other in Miyazaki's canon.

Love Hina   A megahit manga and anime series from the late 1990s by Ken Akamatsu that exemplifies the harem genre — one male character surrounded by a variety of girls who serve as love interests with different characteristics.

Lucky Star   A hit manga and anime series by Kagami Yoshimizu about four high school girls and their everyday lives. It has a fanatical following for its many jokes about otaku topics and culture.

moe   A slang word that describes a particular emotion (pronounced "mo-eh," not like the Stooge). In its original slang usage, the word *moe* describes a character or characteristic that elicits a desire to cherish or protect. For that reason, traditional *moe* characters are often cute, young, or fragile. In wider usage, the term simply refers to things or characters that produce arousal or excitement; in other words, what turns you on. Most uses of the word *moe* within this book are of the latter definition.

Murakami, Haruki   The critically acclaimed author of *The Wind-Up Bird Chronicle* and *Norwegian Wood* (among many others) and unquestionably the most internationally recognized Japanese writer of the last several decades.

Negima!   A megahit manga and anime series by Ken Akamatsu, his first after the conclusion of *Love Hina*. In it, he expands on the concept of *Love Hina* by making the story about a young male teacher (and magician) teaching a class at an all-girls school.

Nico Nico Video   A streaming video website that's similar to YouTube for Japanese users.

NisiOisin   A prominent author of light novels, perhaps best known in the English-speaking world for *Death Note Another Note: The Los Angeles BB Murder Cases*.

"Once again..." The catchphrase of the samurai character Goemon Ishikawa XIII from *Lupin III*. He quotes this line every time he performs a superhuman feat with his sword, such as cutting a helicopter in half.

Ookiku Furikabutte A wildly popular high school baseball manga (the title means "Take a Big Wind-Up") noted for its thorough, in-depth study of the mechanics of the sport. Due to its large male cast and distinct array of personalities, the series has spawned a vast BL dōjinshi following.

otaku An obsessive fan of anime and manga. The term can be affixed to any subject in which a person shows a powerful, geeky interest, such as cosplay, computers, trains, cooking, etc. On its own, however, *otaku* generally refers to members of anime and manga fandom or culture.

relaxed generation The generation that was schooled since the creation of the relaxed education policy in Japan. This policy involved trimming school hours and lowering standards as a response to the extremely stressful classroom environment in the 1970s and '80s, in which school violence exploded. As a result, stress conditions have improved but standardized scores have dropped.

Saikano A sci-fi/romance manga and anime by Shin Takahashi about a normal teenage girl, Chise, whose body has been augmented with extreme weaponry for use in an imminent war. In contrast to the fantastical concept, the story focuses mainly on the fragile emotions of Chise and her boyfriend Shuji at being thrust into this incomprehensible, horrifying conflict.

Sebastian A popular, stereotypical name for butler characters in anime or manga. The trend largely stems from the butler character Sebastian in the classic 1970s anime series, *Heidi, Girl of the Alps*.

seme The "attacker," or dominant member of a homosexual relationship in BL.

Six Codes The six main legal codes that make up Japanese law. They are the Civil Code, the Commercial Code, the Criminal Code, the Constitution of Japan, the Code of Criminal Procedure, and the Code of Civil Procedure.

Slam Dunk A massive hit manga/anime series from *Shōnen Jump*, drawn by Takehiko Inoue. A story about high school basketball players, it was responsible for a massive boom of interest in basketball throughout Japan and other Asian countries.

soba Buckwheat noodles that are roughly the same size as ramen but with a different texture and taste. While they can be eaten in a soup broth like other types of noodles, the traditional way to serve soba (especially in the summer) is on a special tray, chilled. The noodles are then picked up and dipped in a small cup of strong broth (called tsuyu) before being eaten.

Star of the Giants A classic baseball manga/anime series from the 1960s by Ikki Kajiwara and Noboru Kawasaki, it helped establish the possibility of a hit manga/anime property based on sports and extended the popularity of the massively successful Tokyo Giants franchise. In the story, young Hyuuma Hoshi is put through grueling training by his father in order to be a successful pitcher for the Giants. His name, Hoshi, means "star"; thus, the title can also be read as *Hoshi of the Giants.*

Strawberry 100% A romantic comedy manga written and drawn by Mizuki Kawashita and serialized in *Shōnen Jump* starting in 2002. The main character, Junpei Manaka, is surrounded by four girls who correspond to the four cardinal directions — north, south, east, and west.

Sumomomo, Momomo An action/comedy manga and anime by Shinobu Ohtaka. Koushi is the heir of a clan of martial artists, and he just wants to live a normal life. Momoko, also the latest in a long line of warriors, is Koushi's fiancée (against his will)...and very obsessed with bearing his children. Available now from Yen Press!

tsundere   A character archetype referring to people who are normally cold or hostile, but who become markedly warmer or loving in intimate settings. The word is a combination of the adjectives *tsun-tsun* (aloof or combative) and *dere-dere* (love struck).

Twelve Kingdoms   A series of fantasy novels by Fuyumi Ono noted for their rich and elaborate setting reminiscent of Chinese mythology. Also adapted into anime and video game formats.

uke   The "receiver," or submissive member of a homosexual relationship in BL.

Whisper of the Heart   A 1995 animated film by Hayao Miyazaki's Studio Ghibli, in which a bookish girl goes searching for the person whose name is written on the library card of every book she checks out of her father's library.

Whistle!   A soccer manga drawn by Daisuke Higuchi and originally published in *Shōnen Jump*.

yaoi   Media focusing around male-male homosexual relationships for a largely female audience. Within yaoi, the two members of a partnership are referred to as "seme" (attacker) and "uke" (receiver). When characters from an existing story are placed into a piece of yaoi as a romantic pairing, the pairing is labeled with the characters' names separated by a multiplication sign; e.g., Roy x Ed from *Fullmetal Alchemist*.

Y-ko   A popular and slightly jokey method of providing a slight degree of privacy is to replace the bulk of one's name with the initial in the English alphabet, leaving only the last character in place. In this case, "Y-ko" could be a replacement for women's names like Yuko, Yoko, Yaeko, etc. The method is seen often in Japanese because many names — both given and family — end with one of a small number of characters, such as *-ko* for women or *-ta/-da* for surnames.

**My girlfriend is two years older than me...
and she's a fujoshi.**